DISCARDED

Queen OF THE Dead

A GHOST AND THE GOTH NOVEL

STACEY KADE

HYPERION
NEW YORK

Text copyright © 2011 by Stacey Kade

Printed in the United States of America
First Edition
10 9 8 7 6 5 4 3 2 1
V567-9638-5-11074

Reinforced binding
ISBN 978-1-4231-3467-1

Visit www.hyperionteens.com

SUSTAINABLE FORESTRY INITIATIVE

Certified Fiber Sourcing

www.sfiprogram.org

THIS LABEL APPLIES TO TEXT STOCK

To Mom and Dad,
thanks for endless readings of *Go, Dog. Go!*
and *Little House on the Prairie*, all the trips to the
library and bookstore, and not freaking out when
all I wanted to read were stories about ghosts,
witches, haunted houses, and other scary things.
And special thanks for all the phone calls and
Gmail chats this year. Love you guys!

❧ 1 ❧

Will

On television, ghost-talkers run antique stores, solve crimes, or stand on a stage in a nice suit giving the teary-eyed audience a toothy, yet sympathetic grin.

I, however, was entering my second hour of hiding in a prickly tangle of brush with an increasingly cranky spirit guide, all for a ghost who might not even show up.

The Gibley Mansion in Decatur's historic district had been falling apart for years. But it was officially scheduled to be torn down tomorrow morning, which meant tonight was Mrs. Ruiz's last chance to make peace with the place where she'd served as a housekeeper for most of her life. So, we were waiting (and waiting and waiting) for her on the east side of the house, in the former rose garden, where she'd keeled over twenty some years ago while digging a hole for a new bush.

Unfortunately, ghosts don't always do what you expect.

"Can we go now?" Alona nudged me, sounding annoyed. "I have to pee."

Case in point.

I just looked at her. Since she hadn't had anything to eat or drink in well over a month, I seriously doubted that was a genuine concern. Besides which, I hadn't ever heard of any ghosts visiting a bathroom unless, of course, they'd died there. (No, I've never met Elvis, but it's an educated guess.)

Alona tried again. "I'm cold?"

That was at least possible, especially given what she was wearing. Alona Dare, former Homecoming Queen, varsity cheerleading cocaptain, fashionista and mean girl supreme of Groundsboro High, had died in her gym clothes—short red shorts and a cheap white shirt. If you don't believe in karma, that alone should give you cause for reconsideration.

But given that it was an early Monday evening on what had been a blazing hot June day and I could still feel the heat rising from the ground beneath us, she was probably more comfortable than I was in jeans and the long sleeve T-shirt I'd worn to protect myself from rampant thorns.

"Fine." She dragged out the word on an impatient sigh. "I'm dead and I'm bored. How much longer do we have to wait?"

"She'll be here," I whispered. "Soon." I tried to sound more certain of this than I actually was.

"Why are you whispering?" she asked with a frown.

"Because unlike you, *I* can still be arrested," I pointed out.

Apparently fearing that the mansion might be a target for last-minute vandalism or pranks, the city had boarded up all the windows, hung about nine hundred NO TRESPASSING signs, placed caution tape around the entire perimeter, and hired security guards to make regular patrols. We'd slipped onto the property when the guards changed shifts.

Alona waved my words away. "Dopey couldn't catch his own ass if it was on the seat next to him."

She might be right about that. In fact, I was kind of banking on it. Dopey, as Alona had dubbed the security guard on duty, was currently dozing behind the wheel of his rent-a-cop car, which was parked in the driveway about twenty yards away. Loud snores emerged from the open car windows. I just hoped he would keep on snoring until after our business with Mrs. Ruiz was done, assuming she even showed up. Sometimes ghosts, when faced with final resolution of their earthly issues, panicked.

"Did you, by any chance, think to find out what time she died?" Alona asked with just enough sarcasm to suggest she already knew the answer.

"No." Which I could see now had been an oversight. But Mrs. Ruiz had caught me off guard by approaching me at the grocery store. It had been challenging enough to find out what she wanted without freaking out the entire produce aisle, including my mom.

"I would have," she muttered.

"You were unavailable for consultation," I said through gritted teeth.

For somebody who was dead, Alona had an active social life. She was forever dropping in to spy on living family and friends, despite my warnings against that, and attempting to socialize with other ghosts.

The latter, I suspected, had not been going so well. Most ghosts moved on to the light too quickly to concern themselves with making friends while in this in-between place, what I called Middleground. The ones who remained tended to be a little too obsessed with whatever was keeping them here—an injustice, unrequited love, finding their murderer, etc.—to be good company for very long. Trust me, I know—from years of overhearing them.

But I also thought it might be because Alona did not really make friends easily. In life, she'd collected followers. There was a big difference between the two, as she'd found out after she'd died a couple of months ago and had to hear all her former "friends" talking about her.

There were a few ghosts who hung around her—like the sorority girl from Milliken who'd drowned in a hazing accident and now walked around with lake weed threaded through her hair and left wet footprints everywhere. Sometimes I wondered if they thought being friends with Alona would earn them a higher place on the running list of spirits we were trying to help attain closure. Sometimes I think Alona wondered about that, too.

4

But she kept trying, which I had to give her credit for, even though that meant she was gone sometimes when I needed her, like at the grocery store with Mrs. Ruiz. If I didn't know better, I would have suspected she staged her absences deliberately to remind me how much I was dependent on her help to keep the ghosts at bay.

Alona had gotten bounced from the big white light about a month ago, and helping other ghosts who were stuck in-between earned her the karma points, for lack of a better term, to allow her to regain entry someday. At least that was the theory. I got the impression that Alona's sources in the white light hadn't been all that specific. She refused to talk much—at all, really—about her time there. As she told me once, it wasn't like she'd been greeted at the gates by some big guy in white robes and Jesus-type sandals. It was more a feeling than anything else.

Alona shifted impatiently. "Why do we need Mrs. Ruiz anyway? Can't we just go in and get the thing, whatever it is, and bring it to her?"

I shook my head. "She didn't say what or where it was." Mrs. Ruiz's ability to make peace with her past was evidently tied to some object that was still hidden inside the house. "So, unless you want to search under every floorboard and in all the walls—"

She sighed. "Okay, okay."

But she wasn't done yet. I could sense the wheels turning in her mind. Even though we'd gone to school together for years, I'd only known Alona—as in actually having spoken to her—since she'd died. But that was long enough to know she didn't give up that easily.

She stood abruptly.

"What are you doing?" I hissed.

She looked down at me, unconcerned. "What? If we're staying, I need to stretch. We've been sitting here for hours. And Dopey couldn't see me even if his eyes were open, which"—she glanced in the direction of the security guard's car—"they're not."

She reached behind herself and caught her ankle and pulled her leg toward her back, bending forward slightly. Her long blond hair slipped forward over her shoulder, and a wave of her light flowery scent washed over me.

I looked away. Alona Dare had the best legs I'd ever seen. Long and toned, with smooth skin that made you ache to touch them to see if they felt as good as they looked. I'd had fantasies about her and those legs since the sixth grade. And she knew it.

I shifted uncomfortably and kept my gaze locked firmly on a nearby tangle of leaves. "If that security guard sees the branches moving, he's going to come running over here," I warned. Thanks to my "gift," if that's what you wanted to call it, Alona—and all other ghosts—had physicality around me, the same as she would have if she were alive. Dopey might not be able to see her, but he'd definitely notice the bushes moving in a way that didn't look wind-generated.

"He'd have to be awake first," she said back, mimicking my warning tone. Out of the corner of my eye, I saw her switch legs and stretch the other one, giving a small sigh of pleasure.

I swallowed hard. I guess stretching still felt good even when you were a ghost. I know it looked good.

"There. Much better." She sat down next to me again, closer than before. Her shoulder pressed into me, and her leg rested against mine.

Thirty seconds ago, I'd been concerned about nothing other than finding Mrs. Ruiz and getting in and out of the house undetected. Now all I could think about were those two points of contact between us, connecting in a white-hot line of awareness.

I turned to see her watching, so close, so very close to me.

"What?" she asked.

I cleared my throat. "You have a . . ." I reached out and pulled a bit of leaf from her hair. The blond strands slipped like silk through my fingers. I'd touched her hair before, wrapped my hands in it when kissing her, as a matter of fact, and I wanted nothing more than to do it again right now.

"Thanks." Her mouth curved in a knowing smile, and I was lost, even though I knew better.

I leaned closer, drawn to her mouth like it was pulling me in with some mysterious gravity of its own, half expecting her to push me away.

But she didn't. Her mouth was warm and soft under mine.

I sat up straighter without breaking the kiss and slid my

hand to the back of her neck, pulling her closer and slipping my fingers into her hair again.

She moved with me willingly and made that same sound of pleasure I'd heard from her before. I could feel her softness pressing against my chest. Oh, God. She just felt so good.

I pulled back for a second and watched her eyes open slowly. She looked as dazed as I felt, but with a touch of self-satisfaction. She'd planned this, of course.

"So is this when you try to talk me into leaving again?" I asked, breathless. I was all too aware that Alona knew my weak spots and wasn't afraid to use them against me. Not that I minded at this exact moment.

She didn't try to deny it. She leaned in and kissed the edge of my mouth. "Maybe I'm not so bored now."

Good enough.

She rose up on her knees and balanced herself with her hands on my shoulders before laying a series of tiny kisses along my cheek. Her breath was warm, and her eyelashes fluttered against my skin like small caresses. Her scent filled me, overwhelmed me with the desire to shut out everything but her. This girl who equally drove me crazy and made me care about her more than I should. She was the only one who understood. The only one who could help make what I was more bearable, even if she occasionally tortured me in the process.

I slid my hand down her back to her hip, where the edge of her shirt met her shorts. And she let me. More than that, she moved closer, her mouth suddenly hungry on mine. My hand slipped under the hem, and I stroked the bare, warm skin of her stomach with my thumb.

She pulled back sharply, her hand catching mine and holding it in place. "Wait."

I shook my head, trying to think while my body was screaming at me to keep going. "Sorry, I just—"

"No." She squeezed my hand. "I hear something."

I don't care! I wanted to shout, but I swallowed the words.

She let go of my hand and cautiously pushed herself up to her feet to look out and over the tangle of brush that protected us from view of anyone walking by.

"Is it Dopey?" I whispered, taking advantage of her momentary distraction to try to adjust the front of my pants. If I had to run now, I'd be in big trouble.

"No." Her voice held a strange note. "Not him."

"Well, then what—"

She turned to face me, and I realized what I'd heard in her voice was suppressed laughter. The very same thing danced over her expression.

"It's Mrs. Ruiz," she said. "I think." She sounded almost gleeful.

Ah, now it made sense. Because Alona had been off doing whatever when Mrs. Ruiz had approached me, this was her first glimpse of the . . . woman.

"Don't," I told her. "We're here to help."

I stood up, carefully, and peered out to see for myself.

Alona was right. Directly across from us, Mrs. Ruiz

had finally materialized, her garden spade in hand. She was looking around like she was searching for just the right location to dig the hole that would kill her.

"Are you sure it's *Mrs.* Ruiz?" Alona whispered in my ear, clearly delighted.

Okay, so Mrs. Ruiz was not a small woman or particularly... feminine. She was beefy with broad shoulders that belonged on a coal miner. The shapeless but heavily patterned housedress she wore didn't help matters, making her look that much more like a man in drag. The not-so-faint outline of a mustache on her upper lip was a little ... off-putting as well. But still, she needed our help.

"Stop," I said to Alona. Then I eased out from behind the tangle of branches, keeping an eye on Dopey, who, thankfully, continued to snore throatily. Alona followed.

Mrs. Ruiz saw us coming and gave me a curt nod of acknowledgment. She frowned at Alona, which had the unfortunate effect of drawing her two eyebrows into one big one. I could almost feel Alona shaking with the need to spout something spiteful but funny.

"Some people aren't as obsessed with appearances as you are," I said quietly over my shoulder to Alona.

"Yeah, well, I wouldn't be obsessed with my appearance if I were her, either," Alona said, not as quietly as I would have liked.

"This way," Mrs. Ruiz said when we were close enough. She gave Alona another dark look and then slung her spade over her shoulder and started toward the house, ignoring

Dopey and his car like they weren't even there.

"Cut it out," I said to Alona under my breath once we'd passed the security guard and Mrs. Ruiz was far enough ahead on the worn walkway to the front door.

"Oh, come on," she said. "Even you can't blame me for this one."

"I mean it."

She stayed quiet for a second. Then she looked thoughtful. "Ten bucks says she's got a tattoo of an anchor somewhere on her body."

"Alona!" I whispered as loudly as I dared.

"What, you've seen it?"

I glared at her.

"She has a 'stache that would put a porn star to shame—hello, it's called waxing?—and you're lecturing me about—"

I pointed to her feet, which were beginning to flicker in and out of existence, as though a faulty movie projector were involved.

She sighed. "Damn."

A being of mostly energy, she was dependent on keeping the energy flowing by remaining positive, i.e., nice. Which annoyed her to no end, unfortunately. Made for some highly entertaining moments on my end, though.

"She looks very strong and was probably very . . . capable at her job," Alona said carefully. I could see she was dying to make some further remark, like how it was hard to keep a good man down. Or, how handy it was that she could carry the cows around while she milked them, or whatever. "You suck the fun out of everything," she said to me.

It wasn't my rule, just a rule of existence here, but I knew she hated being reminded of it. "Everything?" I asked, taking in her rumpled hair and the way her lips still looked puffier than usual, thanks to our kissing session.

Her cheeks turned pink, but she rolled her eyes and stalked past me to where Mrs. Ruiz was waiting on the front porch.

Nice. I was taking that as a compliment.

I hung back, using one of the huge old pine trees that dominated the front yard to block me from the view of any passing cars, until I saw Alona pass through the heavy wooden door as easily as if it were mist. Once I was sure she was in, I hurried to the porch, where my presence gave her the physicality she would need to unlock and open the door for me.

Except she didn't. Five seconds passed. Then ten. And I was feeling mighty exposed, standing there on the front porch in full view of the road, until the door finally groaned and opened about two feet.

Alona stuck her head out. "Welcome to Craphole Manor," she said with a grimace, stepping back to let me squeeze in.

The front hall was dim and smelled of mold and neglect. The scarred wooden floor seemed pretty solid, at least, but the wall was down to the studs in several places, whether due to predemolition work or decay, I didn't know. I tried to shove the door shut again, but only got it to move a few inches. It had obviously swollen in the last few days of heat and humidity to a point where it no longer truly fit inside the frame. Great.

It would be good to have the fresh air and the extra light beyond the small flashlight I'd jammed in my pocket at the last minute. But anyone looking closely enough at the front of the house would see that the door was open.

"We need to move quickly," I said.

"You don't need to tell me," Alona said with disgust, stepping back and brushing her hand down the sides of her shorts, creating grayish streaks of dust visible even in the limited light.

"Where'd she go?" I asked. "Did you say something?"

"Why are you always so quick to blame me?" she demanded.

"Because it's usually you?" I offered.

"This way." Mrs. Ruiz emerged from the shadows behind us, making both of us jump.

She pushed past us, still carrying her garden shovel, toward what had once been a grand and sweeping staircase. Now, with most of the spindles missing out of the railing and some of the stairs rotted through, it looked more like an eerie smile of broken teeth.

I started to follow her.

"Wait," Alona said from behind me.

I tensed, expecting that she'd heard something from outside, but when I turned, I found her staring into the dark gloominess of the first room to the right of the front door. "What's wrong?"

"Give me the flashlight." I could hear the frown in her voice.

I turned it on and handed it to her.

She swept the beam over the remains of the room. It appeared to have been a study or a parlor of some kind. At the back of the room, a dark doorway to the kitchen or whatever room was next door was a solid patch of inky blackness. Huge rectangular holes dominated the walls where it looked like the built-in bookshelves had been removed. A few scattered, moldering books still lay on the floor along with . . . I frowned and moved closer for a better look.

"What are those?" Alona asked, voicing my exact question.

In the center of the room, five black metal boxes had been placed on the floor in a precise five-point arrangement, each box equidistant from the others. A thick black cord trailed from all of them to what appeared to be a portable generator.

The boxes themselves looked well-worn. The sides were dented and dinged, and the black paint was chipping off in many places. The roughly soldered edges of the boxes looked like nothing that would come out of a factory. Someone had made them.

I shook my head. "Something to do with the demolition, maybe? Explosives or something. Don't touch anything."

She gave an exasperated sigh. "It's not a Vegas high-rise. They're going to tear it down, not blow it up."

I shook my head. Something about this was just off.

"I don't know. Let's just get this done and get out of here before—"

"This way!" Mrs. Ruiz's voice boomed from above, making us both jump. The former housekeeper sounded annoyed, on the edge of angry.

"Does she even know other words?" Alona asked.

"Come on," I said. I took the flashlight back from her and headed for the stairs.

Aiming the light ahead of me, I found Mrs. Ruiz waiting for us at the first curve of the stairs. "This way," she said yet again, sounding a little more relaxed.

"Cute *and* a great conversationalist," Alona murmured behind me. "You really know how to pick them."

"Watch your feet," I muttered back.

"Shut up," she snapped. But then I heard her muttering compliments about the house's original architecture and style—"Real hardwood floors!"—so I knew I'd been right once again.

The staircase creaked and moaned under our weight, but it held, thankfully. At the top of the stairs, Mrs. Ruiz led us down a long dark hallway with doors on both sides. The doors, which presumably led to the family's bedrooms, were open, but only the faintest light seeped out under the boarded-up windows, and I really didn't want to point the flashlight inside any of the rooms. I had no idea what I'd see, if anything, and honestly, even my creeped-out level was on the rise. If I happened to look in one and see some little face staring back at me, I'd probably bolt. Two ghosts were more than enough for now, thanks.

Ahead of us, Mrs. Ruiz stopped at the last door on the right, the only one that was shut.

She looked back over her massive shoulder at me. "This way," she said, at the same time Alona whispered it mockingly in my ear.

Mrs. Ruiz turned the knob and pushed the door open, the loud creak of the hinges echoing in the empty house. She stepped just across the threshold and stopped. The shovel slid off her shoulder, the metal end landing on the floor with a heavy and hollow thud, and her more-than-sturdy frame began to tremble.

Something was wrong.

I eased past her into the room, with Alona just behind me, and the reason for Mrs. Ruiz's distress became immediately clear.

All over the room, random floorboards had been torn up with careless effort, splintering the ancient wood into dangerously sharp spikes. Plaster dust coated the floor from the dozens of recent holes punched or cut into the walls. Clearly, someone had been looking for something.

"Told you," Alona muttered, referring to her plan to come in without Mrs. Ruiz.

I ignored her. "Mrs. Ruiz," I said, approaching her cautiously.

She didn't look up, fixated on the destruction, and I wondered if this had been her room. It would make sense that whatever she wanted would have been in the one room she thought of as her own.

"Mrs. Ruiz," I tried again.

This time, she did meet my gaze, and her fury was enough to make me take a step back.

"You," she said through gritted teeth.

"Hey, a new word!" Alona, who had moved past me to further inspect the damage and possibly the empty closet, piped up.

I kept my attention focused on Mrs. Ruiz. "No. I didn't do this."

But my words had little effect. "Told only you," she said in that gravelly voice, further deepened by rage.

I held my hands out in a peacemaking gesture. "I'm sure it might seem that way, but surely someone else—"

She hoisted her heavy shovel back up to her shoulder, choking up on the wooden handle like it was a baseball bat.

Oh, crap. Another downside of the giving-physicality-to-ghosts element of my gift was that the pissed off ones could use it to try to kill me.

I backed up slowly. "Alona?"

From the corner of my eye, I saw her look up sharply, registering the note of barely repressed panic in my voice.

She sighed and started toward Mrs. Ruiz, stepping over and around the missing floorboards with a grace that made it look like she did it every day. "Okay, look, I know he can be annoying, but he doesn't steal stuff. Believe me."

She gave me an exasperated look. Evidently, she was still irritated that I'd refused to take part in her elaborate plan to get her hands on an iPad. She'd been convinced the touch screen would be sensitive enough for her to use it even when I wasn't around to give her the physicality to do so. Blogging, Twittering, and a Facebook page—all for a dead girl. I don't think so.

"So, there's no need to go crazy," Alona continued. "He didn't take your . . . whatever. Besides, you need to go through me—"

To get to him. Those words had some kind of ritual-like effect, temporarily freezing ghosts who intended me harm. But before Alona could speak, Mrs. Ruiz lashed out with a meaty fist and connected solidly with Alona's face.

Alona is not a tiny, fragile girl. She is athletic, toned, and muscled from years of tough cheerleading workouts and the relentless pursuit of cellulite extinction. But she was no match for Mrs. Ruiz and the power behind that blow.

She flew backward, striking the wall behind her before sliding down into an unconscious heap on the floor.

"Alona!" I lunged for her, Mrs. Ruiz temporarily forgotten. Yes, Alona was, in theory, already dead, but you don't spend eighteen years as a ghost-talker without realizing there are all kinds of dead, and some kinds are preferable to others.

I dropped to my knees in front of her, but before I could touch her, she flickered and vanished.

I pulled back. She'd exhausted her energy on this plane of existence. Alona rarely disappeared completely anymore, having gotten the hang of the positive-energy thing. But every time it happened might be the last, meaning she might not be able to come back.

It would happen someday. It was unavoidable. Alona would be gone, either because she'd disappeared one too many times or the light had returned to get her. The question was, would it be today? I felt sick just thinking about it. I didn't want it to happen like this, Alona sacrificing herself to save me.

The air whistled above my head in a split-second warning, and I threw myself backward as the shovel cracked down where I'd been kneeling. I landed hard on my back, and splinters gouged through my shirt and into my skin. The other immediate question was, without Alona, could I survive Mrs. Ruiz?

I gritted my teeth and forced myself up even as Mrs. Ruiz brought the shovel to her shoulder again. I scrambled for the door, my back protesting and trickles of blood rolling down my skin.

I fell more than stepped into the hallway, just grateful to be out. Then I heard Mrs. Ruiz's heavy step behind me. I pushed myself up to my feet, expecting the crack of the shovel again at any second, this time maybe against my head.

Instead, the doors on either side of me slammed closed, followed by the next two, all the way down the hall.

She was closing me in. Damn, she had to have some serious energy to be shutting doors without touching them. Speed wasn't her strength; *strength* was. If I didn't make it to the front door fast, she might be able to slam that one shut on me, too, and then I'd be stuck. I might be able to kick out the plywood covering one of the windows, but I wasn't sure I could do that before Mrs. Ruiz caught up to me with her shovel.

Panting and gritting my teeth against all my various aches and pains, I hobbled for the stairs as quickly as I could.

At the top of the stairs, the edge of my shoe caught on the rotting remains of the stair runner, and I slipped down the first few steps. I reached for the railing to pull myself up, and Mrs. Ruiz's shovel slammed into the wood, just missing my fingers. Loose spindles rained down on the floor below.

I yanked my hand back with a yelp. "I was just trying to help you, okay? I didn't take your stuff!" I shouted at her.

"I did." A new voice spoke up from below.

I risked taking my gaze off Mrs. Ruiz to aim the flashlight, which I'd somehow managed to hang on to, past the curve in the staircase. A girl I'd never seen before stood at the foot of the stairs, her face pale in the light. Long, dark curly hair floated in a cloud around her head, like it had a life of its own. She was dressed all in black, which helped her blend into the surrounding dimness. Another ghost? Great.

But then I saw she held what appeared to be a flashlight, aimed at the stairs, but it wasn't on, for some reason. In her other hand, she had a dirty old pillowcase, stuffed full of something with hard edges and with considerable weight. The case looked ready to split open.

So, not a ghost then. A thrill seeker? A looter?

The girl shook the pillowcase, and it made a heavy jangling sound, like coins but louder. "Looking for this?" she asked.

"No," I said slowly, but she wasn't looking at me. She was staring at something or someone above my head.

Mrs. Ruiz grunted, and I felt the staircase shake as she started down.

I pulled myself up to my feet and stumbled down the rest of the stairs. I didn't want to be in her way.

When I reached the bottom, the girl's gaze flicked to me for split second before returning to monitor Mrs. Ruiz's lumbering descent. And a delayed realization finally clicked in. This girl *knew* someone else was there. She could see or hear—maybe both—Mrs. Ruiz.

She was a ghost-talker. A real one. Like me.

Holy shit.

"Silver spoons?" The girl shook the bag again. "Really? They left you their mansion and you stole all their good spoons? From more than one set, too."

Still reeling from my discovery about this mystery girl, I forced myself to focus on the conversation going on. That's what this was about? Flatware?

"This place was not a gift!" Mrs. Ruiz shouted. "It was a prison, one I would have escaped when the old woman finally died, but she made me tenant of this place instead of giving me the severance she had promised. I did not own it. I could not sell it. After years of devoting myself to her every need, I still could not leave." Apparently, seeing her recovered hoard had loosened up her vocal cords. Alona would have been impressed.

Mrs. Ruiz slammed her shovel into the banister, like an All-Star player on steroids. The old wood fractured and collapsed. Bits of it sprayed in all directions. She grinned, a horrible, dark expression. She hadn't been protecting the house from unworthy people, as we'd thought. She'd been protecting her stash, her self-awarded reward that she'd never gotten a chance to cash in.

"That must have really pissed you off." The girl gave the pillowcase another heavy shake and began backing up, past the still partially open front door, to the study/parlor room.

The place where Alona had found all that strange equipment.

Suddenly, pieces of this puzzle were falling into place. Whatever that stuff was, Alona had been right. It had nothing to do with the demolition. It belonged to this girl and whatever she had planned for Mrs. Ruiz. We'd obviously interrupted her . . . what? Investigation? Exorcism?

Mrs. Ruiz, her gaze fixed on the pillowcase in the girl's hand, was following her into the room, like a dog fixated on a liver treat. A sterling silver liver treat.

As the former housekeeper passed me, I moved to follow, even as aching and bloody as I was. I had to see what was going to happen next, once the girl got her into that room.

That was a mistake.

Mrs. Ruiz, evidently deciding that the girl and I were in on this together or that my continued existence was just another affront she could no longer stand, spun around at me with her shovel. I dropped to the ground, flashlight skittering from my numb fingers.

She missed me, but I felt the rush of wind over my head when the shovel passed. And there was nothing to stop her from another attempt now that she had her sights on me. The front door was only about five feet away, but Mrs. Ruiz was much closer.

From the corner of my eye, I saw the girl jerk her flashlight upward.

A bright blue beam emerged from the device, catching Mrs. Ruiz in the right side.

Rage contorted her face, and she angled her body as if to take another swing at me. I flinched away in anticipation. But even as I watched, her fingers twitched around the handle of the shovel, but neither the shovel nor her arm moved. She tried again and again, with increasing panic. The beam seemed to hold her in place where it touched her.

I let out a breath of relief.

Then she reached for me with the hand that was not caught in the beam. Her gnarled and dirty fingers scraped past my nose.

"More to the left," I shouted at the girl. She swore under her breath and corrected her aim quickly.

The beam encompassed the entire ghost, and Mrs. Ruiz froze. Then her mouth dropped open in a silent scream. A loud buzz filled the air, and I could feel the hair on my arms stand up.

The light grew brighter for a second, and then Mrs. Ruiz vanished with a pop that made my ears hurt.

The girl cut the beam off immediately, letting loose a torrent of swear words almost as vicious and painful as the pop that had preceded them.

"What was that?" I asked, still stunned.

"That was you screwing up my life. Thanks." Then she turned on her heel and speed-walked into the room with the equipment.

I scrambled to my feet, grabbing my flashlight from where it had fallen, and followed her more slowly. I watched as the girl gathered up the metal boxes from the floor, yanking the cords out and shoving everything into an enormous black duffel bag she'd produced from somewhere.

"I'm serious. What was that?" After a beat, I realized there was a better question. "Who are you?" The only other ghost-talker I'd ever known had been my dad. And he'd died—killed himself—three years ago. I'd always assumed there were probably more of us, as rare as we seemed to be. It was, after all, passed down through families. I couldn't be the only one out there to hit the genetic lotto, so to speak. But I'd figured that most of them were either crazy or dead, given that I'd been on one or both of those paths myself until recently.

"I'd get out of here if I were you," she said. "Ralph is too scared to come in here on his own, but he'll call for backup." She slung the now full bag over her shoulder, and headed toward the door to the next room, lugging the generator with her. The pillowcase of silverware and the flashlight device that had saved my life were nowhere to be seen. Maybe they were in the bag as well?

"Ralph . . ." I had no idea who she was talking about.

"The security guard?" she asked with disdain.

As she spoke, I heard the rising sound of sirens from outside. *Damn.*

"Wait. Tell me who you are, how I can find you." I couldn't just let her walk away without knowing *something*. Everything I knew about being a ghost-talker had been pieced together from bits of information my dad had reluctantly let slip, and what little realistic information I could find in books and on the Internet. Most of it was very woo-woo, spiritual crap, nothing very practical. The chance to compare notes, to learn from someone else like me, would be huge. And then there was the weapon she'd used on Mrs. Ruiz. If I had one of those . . . suddenly I could picture a life where I didn't always have to be on guard.

She turned, exasperation written on her face, and then something else . . . fear. She dropped the generator and her bag with a speed that surprised me, and whipped the flashlight device from one of the many pockets on her cargo pants.

"Walk toward me," she commanded. "Now."

A flutter of movement to my right caught my attention, and I looked over, half expecting to see Mrs. Ruiz again. Instead, I recognized the vague shape of Alona rematerializing, an indistinct blur of blond hair, white shirt, and red shorts.

Thank God. I let out a breath of relief on multiple counts. "It's okay. She's a friend."

The girl looked at me with a mix of pity and disgust. "You're a Casper lover."

I stared at her. "A what?"

She shook her head and put the device back in her pocket. "Idiot," she muttered.

But I didn't even know enough about what was going on to contradict her.

She scooped up her equipment again and started to walk away. Then she stopped with a sigh. "If I leave you here, you're going to get yourself arrested, aren't you?"

Uh . . .

"Let's go." She gestured at me impatiently. "I can't risk you blabbing to the cops."

"You've got another way out?" I asked. From what I'd seen, the whole house, other than the front door, was locked down and boarded up tightly.

She smirked. "You don't?"

She hustled through the darkened doorway to the next room, leaving me to scramble after her.

❦ 2 ❦

Alona

*D*isappearing sucks. It's literally becoming nothing—simply not existing—for an undetermined amount of time. And that just can't be good by any measure.

But occasionally, reappearing is worse. As Will's official spirit guide, I always reappear next to him, usually about a foot and a half to his right. But I never have any idea how much time has passed, and if he's moved since I was last present, I might be in a completely different location than I last remembered. Which, frankly, is more than a little confusing.

And every once in a while, just to make things interesting, I find myself in the middle of chaos.

"Come on, let's go." Will grabbed my arm as soon as I was solid enough for him to do so, and started pulling me along.

"Go where?" I asked the back of his head, which was liberally coated with dust, turning his black hair gray and dulling the gleam of the earrings in his left ear.

We were now downstairs, I could tell that much. I was pretty sure we were in the room that had held all the strange equipment, although it was gone now. Crap. How long had I been out of it? I could hear police sirens outside, and they were getting closer. "What happened?"

Will ignored the questions and tugged me through the darkened doorway on the other side of the room, the beam from his flashlight dancing and bobbing in a vaguely nauseating manner.

And then a flash of movement ahead of us caught my eye. We were not alone.

"Mrs. Ruiz?" I asked. Oh, she and I were going to have words. Most definitely. I mean, what the hell? We had been trying to *help* her. And there was just no excuse for cold-cocking someone like that. It was a bitch move.

"No," Will said. He sounded grim, but there was also this weird thread of excitement in his voice.

He let go of me long enough to steady the flashlight and focus it on the person ahead of us.

It was a girl, someone I'd never seen before. And yes, I know her back was to me, but with her shabby-looking black cargo pants with the pockets stuffed to the bursting point, boots that looked like army-surplus rejects, and a mass of dark wavy hair on the edge of frizz, I would have remembered her. And scheduled an intervention. Her hair was just screaming for conditioner and possibly a deep oil treatment. She was also carrying the largest duffel bag I'd ever seen, with one of the larger pieces of equipment in her other hand.

"I don't know her name, but she's like me," he said in an undertone.

"Alive?" Duh. I could tell that much by the way she moved, too aware of edges and corners. When you can pass through that kind of stuff, you stop paying as much attention to it. Unless, of course, you're around Will often enough. I'd lost count of the times I'd barked my shins on coffee tables and banged my elbows on doorways as I moved in and out of the field around him that gave me physicality.

"No, a ghost-talker," he said. His gaze, fixed on her, was bright with interest.

Well, that explained it. People who could legitimately see and hear spirits were few and far between. Even fewer still were the ones who managed it without going completely insane. The only other one I'd even heard about was Will's dad, who'd killed himself a few years ago, when the stress of it all had gotten to him. Not exactly a great example to follow.

Still, I didn't like the way he was looking at her, like she was some kind of miracle delivered to his door. So she could see spirits. Big deal. I could, too.

"Really?" I asked. "She doesn't look—"

The girl stopped and spun around to jab a finger at Will. "If you and Miss Queen of the Dead want to keep chatting until you get caught, please, be my guest. But wait until I'm clear, okay?"

I gaped at her. *Nobody* talked to me like that. Not when I was alive, dead, or anywhere in between. "Excuse me? Just because you dress like a homeless person with the requisite matching hair-care regime does not mean I'm—"

Will stepped between us. "Understood."

She nodded curtly and turned back around to start forward again.

I smacked Will's shoulder and he winced. "What the hell are you doing?" I demanded.

He glared at me. "The police are coming—"

"And whose fault is that?"

"—but she's got another way out," he continued. "So unless you want to wake up in jail with me tomorrow morning . . ."

I shuddered. Wherever he was at 7:03 a.m., my time of death, that's where I ended up. And I had kind of a thing about germs and public places. Yes, I know I'm dead. It doesn't make germs any less disgusting.

"Fine," I muttered.

The girl moved through the dark and dusty rooms without hesitation, even in the poor light. She knew where she was going. Or so I thought until she led us into a dead end, a room near the back of the house with nothing but big boarded-up windows and no door, other than the one we'd used to enter.

Great. "So . . . either she's planning a shoot-out, or just hoping if you stand really still no one will notice." I folded my arms across my chest. I could have left at any time, of course, given enough distance from Will to pass through the wall, but I wasn't inclined to leave him alone again so soon, especially not with HER.

"'She' knows exactly what she's doing and never invited you along anyway," the girl shot back with a glare at me.

"Like I need an invitation to watch you fail," I snapped. My God, she just wouldn't shut up.

She set the one piece of equipment down—a portable generator, according to the label on the side—and then slung her heavy bag from her shoulder and shoved it at Will. "Here. Since you've messed everything up already, the least you can do is be useful."

"Hey!" I said on his behalf. She didn't know him well enough to talk to him that way, not like me.

Will shook his head at me, warning me to stay quiet. Right. Like *that* would happen.

The girl ignored us both, reaching through the broken-out window to the plywood covering it.

I snorted. "You're not going to be able to tear through that with your bare hands—"

With only a small grunt of effort, she shifted the plywood piece until it swung up and to the left. She must have removed the bolts or nails or whatever at the bottom of the plywood and loosened the ones on top until it would swing from side to side. And unless someone walking by happened to see her climbing in or out, they'd probably never notice what she'd done.

Talk about planning. I was almost impressed. But

momentary flashes of brilliance did not excuse wandering around like someone who used a grocery cart as her closet.

Holding the plywood aside with one hand, she reached back and grabbed her bag from Will, lowering it out the window carefully. Then she followed, swinging her legs over the window frame and then hopping down to the ground.

She twisted around to face us again. "Hurry up," she whispered to Will, wiggling her hand impatiently for the generator.

As soon as he gave it to her, I half expected her to let the plywood slide shut and then run from the house and us. But she didn't. She held it open for him, waiting semi-patiently even though he was moving slower than normal. In the waning pale blue light of twilight, I could see for the first time that the back of his shirt was torn and he was bleeding in several places. What all had I missed?

Once Will was on the ground, I leaned forward to start through the window myself. And that's when the girl let the plywood go with a mocking little smile.

I yelped and jerked back an instant before it would have connected with my head.

Oh, she did *not* just do that.

I shoved the plywood aside and scrambled out and onto the ground. It was darker than when we'd gone into the house, but I could see them both clearly. They hadn't gotten far, just a few feet from the window. I stalked toward them.

The girl was adjusting her bag on her shoulder when I might have accidentally bumped into her. Hard.

She stumbled forward, almost toppling face-first to the ground under the weight of everything.

"Oh, sorry," I said sweetly. "Didn't see you there." Ghost-talker or not, you do not mess with me. That is rule one. My dad, who is an excellent corporate negotiator, always says that if you let people walk over you once, they'll turn you into their favorite footpath. Or something vaguely fortune cookie–esque like that.

She recovered her balance and straightened up, shifting her bag back into position. "I don't have time for this," she said with an irritated sigh. She turned to face me with something small, silver, and shiny in her hand. It looked like a flashlight, but it wasn't on.

"No!" Will shouted.

"What is that?" I demanded. "What is she doing?"

"Not now, Alona," Will said tightly. He moved to stand between us. "Let's just focus on getting out of here, okay?" he said to the girl. Behind us, the sounds of heavy footsteps and men shouting inside came through clearly even with the windows boarded up. The police were in the house now.

Her gaze darted toward the house and then back to me. "Whatever," she said. "I'm gone."

"Wait." Will started after her. "I still don't know your name."

Oh, please.

She whirled around. "Look, playtime is over," she snapped. "This was my third chance at a containment. And you screwed it up. Get it?"

"No," he said, sounding baffled.

"Let her go," I said. "We don't need her." Seriously, she was a little shorter than me and not nearly as attractive. And yes, I'm qualified to judge. It's always important to know how you rank against other females in the immediate vicinity. Know your competition. Not that she was. Competition, I mean. I suppose she did have a bit of an exotic appeal with all of that hair, and her eyes might have been pretty if I could have gotten a better look to judge, but aside from that? Nothing. Well, the ghost-talker thing, I guess.

She laughed. "Princess, you have no idea what you need." Why did that sound like a threat?

I tried to move around Will to get at her, but he threw up an arm to stop me, and I didn't want to hurt him further.

"Have a nice life, Casper lover," she said to Will. "Stay out of mine." Then she took off at a quick jog, all of her equipment rattling as she went.

Will took a step after her.

"Oh, no." I snagged his sleeve. "Car is that way." I pointed in the opposite direction of the girl.

He didn't respond, and for a second, I thought he might shake me off and chase her anyway.

Seriously? I felt a tiny squeeze of panic, for the first time in a long while. Would he really do that? Ditch me, Alona Dare, for her, some random girl who just happened to be a ghost-talker?

Oh, I don't think so.

Yes, I could make it out of here on my own just fine, but

that wasn't the point. We were in this together. Period. End of story.

"Hey." I snapped my fingers in front of his face. "Wake up. We need to go."

Finally, he nodded and we started hurrying in the direction of the car. Thank God.

But that didn't stop him from looking back after her every ten seconds, or me from noticing it.

Crap. This would have to be addressed.

❦ 3 ❧

Will

"Ow!" I jerked out of Alona's grasp and away from the tweezers she wielded with maybe just a little too much enthusiasm. "Are you trying to make it worse?"

"You have, like, half the bedroom floor back here," she said with no sympathy. "Besides, even if I was, you'd deserve it," she said.

She'd been beyond cranky with me since we'd left the Gibley Mansion grounds, and admittedly, she might be justified in that . . . to an extent. After the girl just left us standing there, it had been Alona who'd pulled it together and led me out, through the backyard and to the next block over, where I'd parked the Dodge. I'd been reeling still, torn between trying to follow the ghost-talker girl and just getting out of there before I got caught.

36

Alona had had no such qualms. She'd dragged me to the car and then, on the way to my house, made me tell her everything she'd missed while she'd been gone.

Unsurprisingly, none of those details—the silver that had been stolen and then restolen, Mrs. Ruiz's attack on me, the weapon the girl had used against Mrs. Ruiz and almost Alona—had improved her mood.

Now in the bathroom at my house, where first aid was supposed to be happening, she was evidently still mulling over everything and blowing things way out of proportion, in my opinion. Thankfully, my house was currently empty. My mom was at the movies with Sam, her semiboyfriend/boss from the diner where she worked.

"So, she could have killed me with that thing, whatever it was, in her hand?" Alona demanded. "Just wiped me out of existence because she didn't like the way I was looking at her or something?"

I hesitated, beginning to reconsider the wisdom of this conversation when I didn't have enough—or any—facts . . . and when Alona was obviously pissed and in a position to cause me pain. "I don't know," I said finally. "I don't know what the device does exactly, but it definitely did something to Mrs. Ruiz."

Alona removed another splinter from my back with brutal efficiency, and I winced.

"I stopped her before she hurt you," I pointed out through gritted teeth. "It's fine. *You're* fine."

"Oh, yeah, I'm great." She waved the tweezers around. "Your new best friend is a homicidal maniac with mysterious weapons and hair that could be used to remove rust off a bumper."

At least she had her priorities straight. I resisted the urge to point out that since Alona was already technically dead, it wouldn't really be homicide. I do have some sense of self-preservation.

"Look, she didn't know," I said. "As far as she knew, you were another ghost who was going to try to hurt her."

"So quick to take her side," she muttered. She bumped past me to wash her hands at the sink.

I stared at her. "What is wrong with you?"

"You know nothing about her, why she was there, even what all that stuff she had with her does." She scrubbed her hands ferociously under the water. "Do you even know what happened to Mrs. Ruiz? Where she ended up after your friend made her vanish?"

"I—"

"No, you don't," she answered for me. "This girl just waves around her cool toys, and you're hooked. No questions asked." She shoved past me to dry her hands on a towel.

"I don't think it's really an issue since I'll probably never see her again," I said. "She wouldn't even give me her name." Which sucked. Maybe I could figure out some other way to track her down, just to talk, exchange some information.

She turned to face me. "Seriously? You're not actually falling for this, are you?"

"What? Why?" I felt like we were in two completely different conversations . . . or on two different planets.

"First of all, not telling you her name is a form of manipulation. It only makes you want to know it more." She shook her head at me in disgust. "Classic girl move. How do you not know this?" She paused and then said, "Never mind. I forgot who I was talking to."

Nice. Just because I'd spent most of high school avoiding social contact . . .

"Or, it's possible she really didn't want me to know," I pointed out.

"Then why not make something up? How would you know?"

I opened my mouth and shut it without saying anything. That was kind of a good point.

She flipped her hair behind her shoulders and ticked another point off on her fingers. "Second, another ghost-talker, a rare and endangered species according to you, just happens to show up at the same place at the same time as you?" she asked.

"Well, yeah," I said. "It's possible."

"Please. Do you have any idea of what the odds would be on that?"

"No, but it doesn't matter," I argued. "She would have had no way of knowing that I would be there tonight."

"Uh-huh." She sounded less than convinced. "Because no one knew about the demolition tomorrow and Mrs. Ruiz's *issues*."

Apparently, none of us had known the extent of Mrs. Ruiz's issues, but her haunting the place was fairly common knowledge, and the impending demolition—as well as the Decatur Historical Society's doomed efforts to prevent it— had been in the local news for weeks.

I shook my head. "This is crazy. You think this is some kind of elaborate scheme? To accomplish what?"

She threw up her hands. "How should I know? Ask your new girlfriend."

I frowned at her. "She's not my—"

"Anyway, it doesn't matter now whether she meant to find you or not," Alona continued.

"It doesn't," I repeated.

"No. The fact is, she did find you. And if there are so few ghost-talkers out there, do you think they're going to let an opportunity like this pass them by?"

"Who?" I was beginning to wonder if one of us had experienced brain damage tonight. Honestly, I wasn't sure which of us was the more likely candidate at this point.

"The people she's working for," Alona said with exasperation. "Weren't you listening? 'This was my third chance at a containment.' That's what she said."

I gaped at her. "We don't even know what that means."

"I can tell you it means someone else is judging her based on whatever she did or did not do with Mrs. Ruiz tonight. And I don't think it's an international committee of former figure skaters."

She folded her arms over her chest and waited for me to respond.

"Do you think this hard about everything?" I asked, not even sure what else to say. It was distinctly possible Alona had missed her calling in life as a conspiracy theorist. Albeit a better-dressed one than most.

She leaned closer to me. "Homecoming Queen, three years in a row," she said. "Do you think that happened by accident?"

She did have a good sense of people, I would give her that. Most of the time, she just didn't give a shit unless it affected her. Which, in this case, I suppose it did, indirectly.

I waved her words away. "Okay, fine. If she shows up again, I'll make sure to ask her all the dark and mysterious motives behind her appearance."

"Good." She nodded, satisfied.

Jesus.

She turned around and began putting all the first-aid stuff back in the box. "Did you like her?"

I tilted my head, not sure if I was hearing her correctly. "I'm sorry?"

"I said, did you like her?" She kept her back to me. She seemed to be rearranging the contents of the first-aid kit by alphabetical order or size or something. It should not have taken that long to put back tweezers, bandages, and anti-bacterial cream.

"I . . ." My God, there was no good way to answer this. "Yes" was obviously out. She'd detect "No" as a lie immediately. And "I don't know her well enough to know if I like her" was just weak. "I was curious," I said finally.

"How curious?"

Damn, another impossible-to-answer question. I was starting to sweat. "I don't understand what you're—"

"She didn't seem to have a spirit guide. At least not right now." Alona shrugged. "And if she ever had one, he probably deliberately made himself disappear just to get away from her," she added, her mouth tight.

Okay . . . there was a question in here somewhere. I could feel it coming. I had no idea from which direction, though. Leave it to Alona, the most direct person I knew, to broach whatever this was in the most oblique manner possible.

"With that device she used against Mrs. Ruiz, she probably doesn't need one," she continued.

The silence that hung in the air after those words held a slightly different quality, like she was testing the verbal waters and waiting for a "too hot" or "too cold" response.

Ah, wait. Now I was getting it.

Maybe.

"I was just curious," I said cautiously. "Not looking to change things."

"She's alive. Your mother would like that better."

I let out a silent breath of relief. I'd guessed correctly. She was worried I wanted to replace her or get rid of her or something, but in true Alona fashion, she couldn't just say that. Nope, that would be admitting that it mattered.

"My mom is still . . . adjusting," I said.

The ghost-talker thing had been a hard reality for my mom to accept, especially once she got the full grasp of what it meant. A normal life for me . . . would not be so normal, even now. I'd applied to colleges, just like we'd talked about, but so far, nothing but a pile of rejections.

I couldn't say I was surprised. You try explaining a spotty

attendance record, more detentions than a reasonable person would bother counting, a half dozen or so in-school suspensions, and God only knows what kind of notes from a vindictive principal on your permanent record (which, by the way, really does exist and the school does send it out) *without* mentioning "ghosts" or "paranormal ability." There were schools that would probably be fine with me telling the truth—if I wanted to major in crystals or something. But that was not what my mom had in mind.

Add to all of that, the person that I spent the most time with now was a beautiful girl who happened to be a spirit but who was still living (in her own way) and very touchable? Yeah. For some reason, that meant only one thing to my mom—the possibility of me having weird, undead, interdimensional SEX. Right.

I wish.

In any case, my mom had been a little less than welcoming the few times she'd been forced to acknowledge Alona's invisible-to-her presence. But I hadn't realized it had bothered Alona this much . . . or at all.

"She'll get there," I said. "She just needs time."

Alona closed the kit and zipped it shut before turning to face me. "You know I'd find another way, if I had to. I don't *need* you need you." She met my eyes defiantly, daring me to contradict her.

"I know." I wasn't sure how she would help people—earn her points, learn her lesson, or whatever it was she'd been sent back specifically to accomplish—without me, her only point of access to the living, but I knew better than to underestimate her. I'd learned that lesson already. "But this is not . . . I don't think . . ." *Blah, blah, blah. Get it together.* I forced myself to stop and start over.

I took a deep breath. "I've been alone with this ghost-talking thing my whole life," I said, choosing my words carefully. This had serious potential to blow up in my face. "Even when my dad was alive, he wanted nothing to do with it. So, yeah, finding someone else like me is kind of a big deal."

She stiffened.

"But it doesn't change anything," I said. "Not like that."

She looked unconvinced. I hesitated and took it a step further. I grabbed her hand, and she didn't pull it free immediately. That was a good sign, right?

"I don't want to do this—what we do—with anyone else, okay?" I said quickly. There. I felt dangerously exposed and kind of like an idiot, but at least I'd said my piece. God, no wonder Alona danced around these kinds of things.

Her eyes widened, and she pulled her hand from mine.

I winced in anticipation. It was entirely possible that I'd completely misinterpreted her concerns, and now I was so going to hear about it. . . .

She touched my face, her fingers light against my cheek, and then she was kissing me. Her mouth was warm and soft and, as always, tasted vaguely of vanilla lip gloss. Her tongue brushed across my lips, and I could barely think.

Huh. Maybe I should take a chance like that more often.

❦ 4 ❧

Alona

Will Killian is a surprisingly good kisser. I mean you'd never know it by looking at him. He's perpetually pale with scruffy black hair, a seriously questionable wardrobe, and an attitude that makes Eeyore look like a ray of sunshine. One might think he wouldn't have had a chance to get much kissing practice, especially what with most people considering him crazy. And yet . . . wow.

I stopped on the sidewalk outside of Will's house, running a tentative finger over my mouth. His mom had come home before things could get too intense, and I had to get out of his room before she barged in. But my lips still felt puffy in that "I've been thoroughly kissed" way. Some guys seem to have the impression they should try to swallow half of your face. But—color me surprised—not Will. He was gentle and sweet, and yet not at all afraid to step up and take the lead.

I shivered in delight at the thought. At one point, he'd pulled me into his bedroom and . . .

"Just a cozy night in, huh?" a sarcastic voice asked from behind me.

I froze, startled, and then groaned inwardly when I realized I recognized the speaker. She'd found me again. "Jealous?" I asked, turning around.

Liesel Marks stood on the sidewalk a few feet behind me. The streetlight overhead turned her pink polka-dotted prom dress into a shade of white with brighter white speckles. Behind her, as always, hovering on the edge of the shadows, was her longtime prom date, Eric Hargrove. He was dressed in the best of powder-blue tuxedo finery. They looked exactly like what they were: escapees from a prom in the late seventies.

But they hadn't really escaped anything. They were stuck here, in between, just like the rest of us. Liesel and Eric had died in a fiery car crash on prom night, a cautionary tale for high school students everywhere. Well, living ones anyway. I personally couldn't have cared less. Karma is a bitch, and you get what you get when you steal someone else's guy.

"Right," Liesel snorted. "Like I want to be the ghost-talker's pet."

On my very first day as Will's spirit guide, Liesel had been the one to explain, very mockingly, all the downsides to the job. They weren't so bad, mostly. I showed up wherever

Will was at the time of my death or anytime I disappeared. And I could be "called" to him, if he concentrated on it. That was it. But I had no such powers over him, unfortunately.

It was something I didn't like to think about, and since Will knew better than to try to make me heel, it wasn't really worth consideration anyway. Except when Liesel brought it up just to rub it in my face, of course.

"What do you want?" I asked through gritted teeth. Damn it, my make-out high was wearing off.

"We need the medium to do something for us," she said without so much as a backward glance at Eric. He rocked on his heels in the background, his hands stuffed into his pants pockets, looking uncomfortable. I almost felt bad for him, tied to this harpy for all eternity, or at least the foreseeable future, just because his hormones got the better of him. Once again, my rule about not dating someone unless they're worthy of you proves true. You know . . . don't go out with someone you don't really like—or like only for one thing—because you could die and then be stuck with him/her forever. Talk about hell.

"Yeah, I know," I said to Liesel. "I got it. Get Mrs. Pederson to forgive you for stealing her man and doing the nasty with him before getting him killed."

Liesel and Claire LaForet Pederson, who also happened to be the Brit Lit teacher at our former high school, had been best friends growing up, until Liesel had pulled her man-stealing crap and then died. Of course, none of that explained why Eric was still stuck here. Technically, from what I'd been able to gather from Liesel's nonstop yammering at the various times she'd stalked me like this, Claire and Eric hadn't actually been dating. Claire had just called dibs.

Look, I am . . . or I *was* a power player at Groundsboro High. I know the ins and outs of our social hierarchy like I know the contents of my closet. Give me fifteen minutes, and I could probably do the same thing at any other school, too. You have to know who the competitors are, how to make friends . . . and the right enemies. (A good enemy, or frenemy, for that matter, will earn you more cred than you could possibly accumulate with years of just the right clothes, hair, etc.)

But one thing you don't do? Mess with another girl's crush. Yes, it gives you a reputation boost temporarily, and if you end up in a relationship with him (see my best friend, Misty, and my ex, Chris), then most people will excuse it as "true love." But that's risky. And to do it just because you can? Because you're bored, lonely, needing a self-esteem fix? When it falls apart, expect instant whoredom.

Because you've just announced, in so many words, to every girl in the school that you have no intention of respecting the unspoken, agreed-upon boundaries of dibs, and their crushes could be next.

Yeah. Not a good idea. Ever.

"You're like nine hundred thirty-six on the list or something," I said. I'd sent Liesel to the end, just for being a pain in my ass. "As they say, today's not your day and tomorrow's not looking good, either." I was pretty sure Will had that on a T-shirt somewhere.

"You need to move us up," Liesel said sharply.

I pretended to think about that. "No."

"You did it for Mrs. Ruiz," she pointed out in a shrill voice that was just so grating. "You put her right at the top."

"And look at how well that worked out," I muttered.

She frowned. "What?"

Evidently, the undead gossip train, which usually moved with bulletlike speed and accuracy, hadn't reached her with the latest details yet.

I sighed. "Nothing."

"We're running out of time." She touched her feathered and heavily sprayed bangs carefully, making sure everything was still in place. A nervous habit left over from life, most likely, when stuff like the wind messed with your look. Unless, of course, you'd used twelve cans of hairspray.

I narrowed my eyes at her and then at Eric behind her. "You look fine to me." Neither one of them appeared to be in any more danger of disappearing than before. Their forms were as solid as ever.

"Claire started dating someone," she said. "His name is Todd."

I raised my eyebrows.

Mrs. Pederson's divorce a couple of years ago had been legendary, especially after the day she'd shown up to teach, allegedly half-looped on some kind of mood upper. Fortunately, it had turned out to be a Saturday. Unfortunately, more than enough people were in the building—practices, yearbook, detention, etc.—for the rumor to be alive and kicking on Monday.

"So . . . you want to stop her? You can't be happy, so she can't be happy until she forgives you? Will would never go for that." I turned away.

"Whose side are you on?" she called after me.

"Not yours," I said over my shoulder.

"Yeah, I noticed. We've all noticed."

I turned at that. "What's that supposed to mean?"

"All you care about is what he does." She folded her arms across her chest. "We don't even matter to you."

I assumed that the "we" she referred to was the general ghost population of the Decatur/Groundsboro area rather than just Eric and her specifically.

"I'm *his* guide," I pointed out.

"But you're one of us," she shot back.

I shook my head.

"You think you're better than us just because you work for the breather?" she demanded.

"Work *with*," I corrected with an edge. "And no, I think I'm better than you because I *am* better than you." I kept walking.

"You're not alive anymore, you know!" she shouted after me. "Not like he is. And being his guide doesn't make you any closer to it. You need to stop pretending. It's pathetic."

I stopped dead and spun to face her again. "I'm sorry?" She was baiting me, I knew that, and yet I could not stop myself. She didn't know anything; she was just lashing out at what she thought might be a weak spot. And yet, tonight, that one particular area just happened to be larger and more vulnerable than usual.

She moved closer, her dress rustling loudly in the quiet summer night air. "You're no different from the rest of us, except you think letting the medium use you makes you something special."

"Any using going on is mutual, I assure you," I said tightly.

She rolled her eyes. "Really? You think he's going to want you around forever? Someone no one else can see? You *work* for him. The rest of it is temporary. You're just conven—"

I suspected that would have been "convenient," but I launched myself at her before she could finish. We went down in a tangle of tulle in Will's neighbor's yard. God, I hoped Will wasn't watching. But even if he was, I couldn't let this go.

"Don't you see? It's not right what he's doing," she insisted, even as we struggled and rolled in the grass.

"I'm not doing it for him. I was sent back from the light to—"

"You mean, you got kicked out!"

I reached for her throat, to shut off her words and her air. Unfortunately, we couldn't really hurt each other.

"Hey, cut it out!" Eric reached between us and pulled us apart, one hand on the back of Liesel's dress and the other on the collar of my shirt. "You're disappearing."

We both looked down at ourselves. Whole sections of

Liesel's torso were see-through, and my legs were gone from the knee down. Damn it.

"You seem very determined to make up for your mistake, which I admire," I offered begrudgingly.

"I like your hair," she said with equal disdain.

But it must have been genuine, on both of our parts, because the fading out stopped.

"Look, we don't want Claire to be unhappy. Just the opposite," Liesel said quickly as if she thought—correctly—I'd start walking again now that I had my legs back. "We have a very limited window here. She doesn't date very often, and when she does, it hardly ever goes this well. Right now, she's happy and excited about Todd. So, she might be more open, more—"

"Forgiving?"

"Exactly." Liesel nodded like her head was loose on her neck.

Just considering this was breaking about every rule I had about the list of the dead who needed our help—it was totally first come, first served, unless you pissed me off and I sent you to the end, or extenuating circumstances bumped you to the top. No playing favorites.

I had to maintain strong, unbiased order, or they'd be walking all over me to get to Will, and I didn't have the time or energy, literally, to fight them all off.

But Liesel maybe had a point—this time—about Mrs. Pederson's potentially more optimistic mood.

The pissy part of me wanted to tell her to forget it, but

the truth was, if I wasn't a little flexible when needed, I'd lose control just as fast as if I were too relaxed about it. Besides, Daddy always said, the well-timed favor earned more respect than yet another example of being a hard-ass.

Plus, she'd said she'd liked my hair and meant it.

"I'll think about it and let you know," I said. Of course, in the end, it wasn't my decision at all, but I sure as hell was not going to say that now. I knew Will would be twitchy about this one, as he always was when it came to dealing with living people he knew. But he'd graduated. As his former teacher, Mrs. Pederson was no longer really in a position to give him trouble. I might be able to talk him into this one.

"Tonight," Liesel said.

I glared at her. "Don't push your luck. Tomorrow."

She opened her mouth to object and seemed to think better of it, which, frankly, would be a first. "Fine," she said with an eye roll.

"And do not even think about going in there to try to talk to him yourself." I jabbed a finger at her. It would be awfully tempting for her, I knew, with him so close by. It was one thing for Mrs. Ruiz, someone we'd never met before, to approach Will directly with an immediate need. Something different for Liesel to continually harass him.

"I won't," she said with exasperation. "God."

"Because I will put you even farther down the list, behind people who aren't even dead yet." I frowned at her. "How did you find me here?"

We were very careful about not meeting spirits at Will's

house. It was the one place where he could be guaranteed some peace and quiet. And since we weren't omniscient after death any more than we'd been in life, and had significantly less access to a phone book or the Internet, most spirits had no idea where he lived.

"I followed you here a couple days ago," she confessed.

Damn. I was going to have to start being even more careful. One more thing to worry about.

"Don't do that again, and if you tell anyone where he lives, you're off the list completely," I said to her, though I wasn't entirely sure I had the authority to make that decision. "Now go before I change my mind."

But she didn't scurry away as I expected.

She brushed off the front of her dress, though it held no dirt or grass stains. "I meant what I said . . . earlier," she said, keeping her eyes focused on her task.

I bristled.

"You're going to have to pick a side at some point, his or ours." She looked up, a challenge in her gaze.

"I'm on my own side," I said.

She nodded, but I could see she wasn't convinced.

Whatever. I turned and walked away. Like what Liesel Marks thought mattered to me. I wasn't working on her behalf.

Will and I had an understanding. He helped me. I helped him. That was all there was to it, and the only thing that mattered.

* * *

Arguing with Liesel had put me in a less than stellar mood—I mean, who did she think she was, anyway?—so I walked home instead of trying to catch a ride . . . or ten. Trust me, there is nothing more frustrating than sliding into a car to hitch a ride only to have it turn thirty seconds later in a direction you don't want to go.

But by the time I breezed through the front door of my old house—literally *through*; this passing through solid stuff thing was awesome so long as Will wasn't around to trip me up—I was feeling better.

Home, for all that it had been a chaotic nightmare when I was alive, was sort of comforting now in its familiarity. School was out. My friends (and enemies) had graduated. I was dead.

But home was still home, you know? The one thing that hadn't really changed.

The downstairs was empty. The lights were on in the kitchen, but my mom wasn't there, which was kind of weird. Now that she wasn't drinking anymore, I usually found her in the kitchen eating a Lean Cuisine right out of the black microwaveable tray while she watched a lame sitcom or chatted online with her old college friends. (I know; creepy, right? The elderly have invaded Facebook. That is just wrong in so many ways.) Pretty much the rest of the time, she was either at an AA meeting or working. She'd gotten a job at the Clinique counter in Von Maur and got to wear one of those cool white lab coats.

"Hello?" I called more for my peace of mind than

55

anything. Occasionally, I still had trouble with the idea that I was in the world but not of it, if that makes sense. It was comforting to keep up the habits and conventions of the living.

There was no answer, of course. But I thought I heard her moving around upstairs.

Our house is a big, brick two-story with a dramatic foyer open to the second floor and a sweeping staircase in the front hall, which, let me tell you, would have rocked for prom photos if I could have ever brought anyone to my house.

I started up the steps, noting that all the piles of magazines, laundry, and school stuff I'd stacked on the individual stairs during the last days of my life had disappeared. Also, very weird.

At the top, I discovered the light was on in my room, and my heart started to pound like crazy. (Yes, I am dead. Yes, I attended my funeral and watched them put my body in the ground. But I still *feel* things. My heartbeat, breathing, laughing, crying, all of that. I can't explain it and don't really even want to try. Just call it Phantom Body Syndrome or something.)

I'd been dead and living, if you can call it that, as a spirit for about two months now. In that whole time, the door to my room at my mother's house had stayed closed. Just like I'd left it when I'd bolted out the door for school on that last morning. Okay, yeah, my mom had probably looked in there every once in a while or whatever. I definitely had. It was kind of disturbing and sad in some way that I didn't quite understand. I mean, I'm still me, I'm still here. And yet, when I'd see my sleep shorts still on the bed where I'd tossed them, the covers shoved back, like I'd just gotten up, and my backup outfit for the day—a super cute vest with matching tie over a three-quarter-length sleeve, white fitted shirt and a black pleated mini—hanging on the front of the closet door, it gave me this odd pang in my chest.

It was like a memorial—or a museum display—for a girl who no longer existed. And yes, while a little creepy, it was also reassuring, like hard proof that I'd once been here and that I might still somehow walk back into my life, into this moment frozen in time.

But now . . . with the door open, the light on, and sounds of movement coming from inside my room, any hint of reassurance was being replaced by blind panic. What was she doing in my room? That was unacceptable. I'd spent years training both my parents to stay out unless they were invited in, which, hello, like that was going to happen.

I bolted the last few steps to my room, a protest she wouldn't be able to hear already forming on my lips, and then stopped dead in the doorway, my mouth falling open.

My mother was not just poking around, picking up random items and crying, as you might expect. Nor was she looking for my secret diary. (I didn't have one—too risky. Why give a rival everything she needs to take you down in one easy package?)

No, my mother was in the middle of my room with a HUGE black garbage bag in her hand, and she was throwing things away! My life was being tossed into the garbage! As I watched, she pried the Krekel's takeout cup of Diet Coke off my dresser, where it had been disintegrating into a puddle of sludge and paper pulp for the last eight weeks or so, and tossed it into the bag. That cup might not seem important to her or to anyone else, but it had technically been my last meal, or part of it.

"What are you doing?" I demanded, when I could breathe again.

"It's not everything. Just the garbage."

I stared at her for a long second. She hadn't heard me . . . had she? No. When I looked closer, I noticed the awkward tilt of her head and her cell phone wedged between her shoulder and her ear. So getting rid of the accumulation of my life wasn't even worth her full attention? Now I was pissed.

"Stop!" I strode across the room and swatted at the bag. My hand passed through most of it—not exactly a shock there—but it jumped a little bit in her hand, which was about the most I could accomplish on my own. She looked down at the bag with a frown. Then, the phone conversation distracted her again.

"No, Russ, I promise. I wouldn't do that."

Russ. My dad. My mother was talking on the phone with my dad? My knees felt wobbly, all of a sudden, like I might faint. I didn't know if that was possible in my condition, but I wasn't eager to find out.

My parents hadn't spoken willingly to each other and

without a third party present in *years*. And somehow I seriously doubted that this was a three-way call with their attorneys.

What the hell? I sank slowly to the floor, next to my mother's feet and the garbage bag. I could see the top of the ridiculous collage I'd been forced to make for Mrs. Johnson's psychology class—theme: How Sex Sells in Advertising—sticking out of the bag's opening.

"It's better. Not easy, but better." She took a deep breath. "Every step helps." Alcoholics Anonymous; she had to be talking about her meetings. My mother had been a hopeless and helpless alcoholic since my parents' divorce three years ago. Which was another reason why this conversation was hitting the top of the freaky-meter. She was actually sober. Stone-cold sober, as far as I could tell. Prior to the last couple of months, my mother had been the queen of drunk dialing . . . and drunk texting, drunk e-mailing, and even drunk drive-bys. Not good.

"I appreciate you letting me know so I didn't have to find out from someone else." She dusted off her hand on her sweatpants and pulled the phone from between her shoulder and her ear and sat on the edge of my bed. Then she took a shaky breath and forced a smile. This close to her and with her face washed clean of makeup, I could see all the little lines at the corners of her eyes. "Congratulations to you and Gigi. Really. It's something to celebrate. I know Alona would be pleased."

A foreboding chill swept over me. Nothing involving Gigi,

my dad's second wife and former administrative assistant, could have possibly pleased me. My mother had become a pathetic, alcohol-soaked mess after the divorce, yes, and I'd spent some time blaming her for my death. I'd been coming home, after dipping out on zero-hour gym, to drag her sorry, hungover butt out of bed so she could meet with my dad (and their lawyers) when the early morning band bus and I had met in a rather sudden fashion.

But Gigi . . . she was just a bitch. When I'd been alive, she'd constantly been after my dad to cut back on his alimony and child support, so she could have more of what *she* wanted. We had a well-documented and mutually understood hatred for one another. Anything she'd celebrate clearly meant trouble for me.

My mom hung up the phone without waiting for a reply. Her face crumpled, and she dropped the bag to pull herself onto my bed, her knees tucked up to her chest. She cried for a couple of minutes into my pillow, which I knew from my last visit had already begun to smell like dust and disuse instead of Pantene and cucumber melon body lotion.

Then she sat up, and to my shock, instead of heading downstairs to stare longingly at the now empty liquor cabinet or to root out the last stash of booze I was sure she had tucked away somewhere, she stood up and grabbed the garbage bag again and began throwing away more of my belongings, muttering under her breath what sounded suspiciously like a prayer.

There went the printout of my painstakingly created

spreadsheet, which compiled all the potential outfit possibilities from the contents of my closet and tracked when I'd worn each combination last. The ticket stubs from when my best friend Misty and I went to the Boys Like Girls concert last October. The tiny scrap of stiff satin I'd cut from the back of the Homecoming Queen sash before returning it that last time. (Yes, they recycled the sash from year to year. That's why there was never a year printed on it. Tacky and cheap, that was Groundsboro High for you.)

I felt like I might throw up. Those things weren't garbage. They were memories, symbols of the life I'd lived, and the only things I had left from it. "Mom! Stop!" I reached for the bag again, with even less success this time. The bag didn't even move.

My protest passed unnoticed, and she continued to crumple up and toss away my most prized possessions. By the time she was done, it would no longer be my room. Sure, she'd leave the furniture, the framed pictures (one of each of my parents, a couple of Misty and me, and various boyfriends at proms and homecomings), my alarm clock and stereo . . . all that stuff would stay.

But the things that had made it mine, really mine? She was chucking them away, like they meant nothing. Like *I'd* meant nothing. Weren't parents supposed to keep all your stuff forever? All those macaroni necklaces, finger paintings, and first spelling tests? Weren't they, like, treasures of the past or something? Wouldn't all of that be even more poignant if your kid was dead?

Watching my mother's efficiency with the garbage bag, it didn't seem like it.

An unwelcome idea intruded. *Will was right.* He'd tried to warn me about this, and I'd ignored him. I brushed that thought aside, fleeing my room and the house. I didn't have to stay here and watch this. She wasn't, thank God, my only parent. She wasn't even my favorite.

Fifteen minutes later, after cutting through backyards, navigating steep drainage ditches, and crossing a few busy streets (another nice thing about being dead—if you've been run over once, you never have to worry about it happening again), I stood at the foot of the driveway to my dad's new house, a little Cape Cod cutesy-bungalow type thing that he shared with Gigi. And it really wasn't so new. It had been three years since he'd left my mom, and two and a half years since he and Gigi had gotten married.

I noticed with a start that the adorable silver VW Eos, my intended graduation present, no longer held a place of honor at the top of the drive, blocking the half of the garage my dad used to store his golfing equipment. Instead, this ginormously ugly minivan had taken its place.

No, no, no. I didn't stop to think, just ran for my dad's study, not even bothering to pass through the doorway. Doors, walls, they were all the same now anyway.

I found my dad exactly as I'd expected and hoped. He was slouching at his desk, his head propped up by his hand, and staring at a photo of us from a Daddy-Daughter Dance in fifth grade. At that time, I'd not yet learned the magic of smoothing crème for taming the frizzies and I still had braces, ugh. But he seemed to like it. It was the only photo on his desk, the only one in the whole room, as a matter of fact. A glass of brandy sat in front of him, inches from his hand. And even in the dim imitation Tiffany-lamp light, I could see that he'd been crying.

"Thank God." I flopped down on the leather sofa behind him, flipping my hair over the armrest so it wouldn't get all tangled, more out of habit than necessity. "Someone still misses me." My dad and I had always been closer anyway. "Do you know what Mom is doing?" I asked. "You have to stop her."

He didn't respond, of course, and even if he, by some miracle, had been able to hear me, I seriously doubted I'd have been able to convince him to go over to her house, his former house, for any reason. He'd left there like he was fleeing a plague-infested city. Going back would be a death wish . . . execution courtesy of Gigi.

But I still felt the need to try. "She doesn't get it, Daddy. She's throwing away everything." To my horror, I felt tears welling up in my eyes and a lump in my throat. In my life, when I was actually living, I'd rarely cried, if ever. Tears were a weakness, a luxury you couldn't afford if you wanted to remain in power. I had, once upon a time, ruled at the top of Groundsboro High society. Now I was dead, and almost everyone I knew had graduated. And I was freaking crying . . . again. My afterlife sucked.

The door to the study opened without a knock, and I sat

up, wiping under my eyes. Gigi. My step-Mothra, so dubbed because she is an evil creature destroying everything in her path, stood in the doorway. Even though she couldn't see me, I didn't want there to even be so much of a hint of vulnerability in the air around my stepmother. Gigi would score no points on me, even in the afterlife.

She made a sound of disgust and then stalked over to my dad's desk and slapped down a piece of paper. "I was going to wait to show you this, but you obviously need something to hold you together." She stepped back, still dressed in her work clothes: trim little black-and-white cropped jacket, a black pencil skirt, and killer patent leather stilettos. Yes, I hated her, but that did not mean I could not respect her ability to recognize fine fabrics and a rockin' pair of heels. It did, however, mean that I could notice with some evil glee the way her skirt was pulling up and straining at the seams, like her ass was a prisoner slowly trying to bust its way to freedom.

"Gigi gi-ant ass." I snickered. *Love it.* Out of habit, I looked down at my hands, just in time to see my fingertips start to flicker. *Damn it.* "But she seems to make my dad happy," I said dutifully.

My father stared for a long time at the paper Gigi had given him, and then he held it up to the light on his desk with a shaking hand. He needed glasses—everybody knew it but him—he was just too vain to admit that it was his eyes rather than the world that had gone blurry. God. Shoot me if I get like that when I'm old. Oh . . . never mind.

"Is this accurate?" he asked in a hoarse whisper. "What it says at the top?"

I sat up a little straighter. From my perspective, over my dad's shoulder and to the side of Gigi's ever-expanding backside, the paper he held looked like one of those abstract, blobby things Dr. Andrews used to try to get me to identify in our completely useless sessions. (I'd just told him everything looked like handbags, varying the designer to keep things interesting. Apparently Steve Madden means I'm suffering from severe repressed hostility.) Only this page was mostly black with a white shape instead of the other way around. But my dad had certainly recognized it, whatever it was.

Gigi sniffed and nodded.

Sniffed? Was she *crying*? I pushed myself off the sofa and moved in for a closer look at whatever this was that could have provoked such a reaction from my step-Mothra, taking care not to bump into my dad or Gigi. I would pass right through them, and while they might shiver at a touch of cold that would be blamed on a random draft, I'd be treated to a stomach-rolling and head-spinning blast of dizziness.

Even inches from the paper, I still had no idea what I was looking at. It looked like a grainy photograph of some big white blur with little arrows and tiny corresponding letters pointing out—I squinted, leaning farther over my dad's shoulder—feet, heart, spine, and . . . *Oh, shit.* There, at the top of the page. *Baby Girl Dare. Due Date: 12/24.*

Gigi was growing my replacement.

I stumbled back and my elbow crossed through Gigi's

chest. She shivered, and I fell to my knees, trying to breathe, and fighting the urge to retch while the room spun around me. A baby? Step-Mothra was reproducing? But my dad had always said he was done with kids. Too expensive, he'd claimed, and besides, what did he need with another one when he had a perfect one already? That's what he used to say to me when Gigi was bitching and moaning about her decrepit eggs.

"A daughter," my father said weakly.

Gigi nodded again. "I know it's not the same. But you've been having such a hard time with the idea of a baby, and while nothing can ever bring Alona back, I thought it might help in some way."

"Help?" I shouted at Gigi. "How can that help?" I staggered to my feet. "You can't substitute one person for another! You can't just switch me out with an . . . imitation of the real thing, like one of your cheap-ass Gucci knockoffs. He's my father. He knows the difference. He knows what you're trying to do and it's never going to work. I'm the only one." I could hear myself losing control and getting a bit hysterical, which would lead to more disappearing body parts. And sure enough, when I looked down my hands had disappeared, along with my feet and ankles.

Calm down. Breathe. If I lost control now, after the hit I'd taken from Mrs. Ruiz earlier, I'd vanish and probably be gone until tomorrow morning . . . at best.

I clamped my mouth shut and waited breathlessly for Daddy's infamous temper to kick in, for him to shout at her for even implying that anything could make the loss of his only daughter more bearable.

Instead, he wiped his face with the back of his hand, and I watched in horror as he propped the ultrasound picture against the framed photo of the two of us, blocking me out entirely except for the top of my ultrafrizzy head.

"Daddy," I whispered. "No."

He beamed up at step-Mothra and pulled her in close, burying his face in what I realized now was an expanding waist. "I can't wait." His voice was muffled, but the broken joy in his voice was very clear.

And my last thought before I disappeared for the second time today was this: my half-sibling was still practically microbial, barely more than a handful of cells, and already she'd beaten me. Unacceptable. This was war.

❧ 5 ❧

Will

I couldn't fall asleep right away. Not for the obvious reason, either.

Well, okay, maybe that was part of it. I could still smell the flowery scent of Alona's shampoo on my pillow and imagined I could still feel the heat of her against me.

But there was more.

Not five minutes after Alona had vanished through the far wall of my bedroom, my mom had poked her head in my room to say good night, and let's face it, probably check up on me.

Her face was glowing with happiness. She must have had a good time with Sam at the movies. Where I was absolutely sure they did nothing but actually watch the movie, and refused to believe any evidence to the contrary. It was too . . . weird.

"Just wanted to say I'm home," she said, beaming at me. My God, was that red patch on her chin stubble-burn? No, no, I wasn't looking.

"Right on time for curfew," I said instead, even though I actually had no idea what time it was.

"Ha, very funny. Good night." She reached for my door to pull it shut again.

"Wait." I hesitated. I didn't want to destroy her good mood, but I had to know.

Of all the crazy stuff Alona had spouted earlier about the other ghost-talker, one part of it had actually made sense.

If there was one ghost-talker around here, maybe there were more.

"Did Dad ever say anything about anyone else? Like us, I mean?"

Her smile faded a bit. "Honey, I didn't even know what was . . . special about him until you told me about your . . . gift."

Nice avoidance of the words "wrong" and "problem," Mom. "No, I know, but did he ever have any visitors or talk about people who weren't from work or whatever?"

She was quiet for a long moment. "Your father was a complicated man, dealing with many . . . troubles."

Like allowing himself to be misdiagnosed as schizophrenic instead of just a guy who could see and hear the dead.

"When he was having a tough day, I didn't want to make it worse by asking questions," she said.

I remembered that—Dad coming home from work early, and my mom hushing me as soon as I walked in the door from school. On those days, the house had to be as quiet, dark, and still as possible. I never really put it together until recently that he needed the peace and quiet because he'd probably spent the whole day trying to tune out all the ghosts he encountered through coworkers and the various locations he had to go to for work. It would have been miserable. At least when I was in school I'd had a rough idea of which ghosts were around, what they might do, and how aware they were or were not of the living, and in particular, me. For him, working as he did, on assignment from the railroad company, he'd have always been encountering new spirits and new problems.

"When he was having a good day," my mom continued, "I . . . I didn't want to ruin it. I'm sorry. That must seem horribly selfish to you now." She gave me a rueful smile, and her eyes were watering.

I winced. "Mom . . ." I started to get up.

But she stopped me, holding her hand up. "I'm fine." She cleared her throat and blinked back her tears. "He wasn't always like that, though. He used to be happier, more social. In fact, when you were much, much younger, he was forever taking off for a weekend 'with the guys.'" She laughed. "He called it book club, though what kind of book club involves coming back exhausted and all banged up, I have no idea.

They were probably off paintballing or some other rough-housing nonsense they didn't want the wives to know about." She gave a laugh tinged with sadness and stared off in the distance at a memory I couldn't see. "I used to get so mad at him."

Then she edged closer to squeeze my foot through the covers. "Just because you're different doesn't mean you have to be alone, sweetie."

Oh. *That's* what she thought I was worried about. Better than the truth.

"I know," I said.

It was her turn to hesitate. "That's why I think it might be a good idea for you to branch out, spend some more time with your other friends." She smiled a little too brightly.

In other words, not Alona.

I could have explained that my other friends were a bit scarce these days, never having been plentiful in the first place. Joonie was still adjusting to living at the group home, not to mention keeping up with the summer classes that would let her earn her high school diploma. Erickson was in California with his cousins for one last summer of surf and smoke, and Lily . . . well, Lily was exactly where she'd been for the last ten months. In a coma at St. Catherine's.

Her soul was gone, having moved on to the light immediately after the car accident that landed her in the hospital in the first place, but her body was still basically functional. A couple months ago, Alona had saved my life by making it seem as though Lily were communicating from beyond (long story). She'd spelled out a message on a Ouija board, and even managed to put her hand inside Lily's for a moment to move it. Since then, her parents had backed way off from the idea of removing her feeding tube and letting her fade. At least, her mom had. I wasn't sure her dad was convinced. I'd visited a few times since that incident, and the tension between them was enough to keep those visits very short. If Lily had been aware and able to, she'd have walked out herself, I was sure of it. Her mother had hovered, always making sure a Ouija board was right at Lily's lax fingertips. Her dad had looked ready to burst a blood vessel every time her mother even mentioned "communicating."

But rather than getting into all that with my mom, who knew pieces of it, but not everything, it was just easier to agree. "Sure," I said. "No problem."

She smiled, pleased at having helped, I'm sure. "I've got an early shift tomorrow. You'll come by for lunch? I think Sam's got you scheduled for the afternoon."

Now that school was out, I was picking up a few hours at the diner as a busboy. The work was not glamorous, but the gas money was good. On days that my mom and I both worked, I usually went in early to eat so I didn't have to worry about fending for myself around here.

"Yeah," I said. Alona would not be pleased. She hated hanging out at the diner. Claimed she could smell the grease in her hair for hours afterward. Again, highly unlikely, but who was I to say?

My mom nodded and started to leave.

"Hey, Mom? The book club guys ... they were from Dad's work?" I asked. It was probably nothing, but I had to ask.

"What? Oh. Actually, I don't know." She frowned. "I don't remember. I think so. It was so long ago, I'm not sure." She narrowed her eyes at me. "Why? You don't think they were ... like *that*, do you?"

Like the girl from the Gibley Mansion? Like me, Mom? "No," I said. Because if so, why hadn't my dad ever mentioned them to me? It was one thing to refuse to talk much about the gift/curse we both shared. A whole other thing to let me think we were alone in it when he knew otherwise. "Definitely not."

She nodded again, seemingly reassured, a spark of her Sam-induced happiness returning. "Good night, hon." She snapped the light off and shut my door on her way out. After a few seconds, I heard her running water in the bathroom and the sound of her footsteps heading down the hall to her bedroom. A few minutes after that, nothing but that heavy silence that comes with someone sleeping.

I wished it could be that easy for me. But my mind would not slow down, playing back the evening over and over again, in fast-forward, rewind, slow motion, and every possible combination. No additional answers emerged, though.

I was finally starting to doze off when a funny scrabbling noise sounded at the window behind my headboard.

My first completely illogical thought, half-asleep and

fuzzy-brained as I was, was that Mrs. Ruiz had managed to pull herself back together, and she was pissed and coming after me. I knew for sure it wasn't Alona. She always managed to slip in and out of the room without a sound.

I bolted up and off the bed, swallowing back the instinctive and childhood urge to call for help, fumbling and flailing to reach the light on my desk.

The window squeaked upward, and I cursed myself for always leaving it unlocked.

I snapped the desk lamp on and hoisted it above my head as a makeshift weapon, just as a familiar face, surrounded by mass amounts of wild dark hair, appeared in the opening. "Thank God," the girl from the Gibley Mansion said, bracing herself in the window frame.

I didn't move, couldn't move. I wasn't entirely sure I was awake.

"You know just about every spook in town knows your name, but not where you live?" Without waiting for a response, she clambered in and stepped down on my bed and then the floor. "What are you doing?" she asked with a frown, taking in the lamp with her gaze.

Like I was the one where I wasn't supposed to be. I couldn't have been more surprised if Jessica Alba had suddenly appeared in my bedroom. Thankfully, I'd thrown a T-shirt on after Alona had left, and getting caught in boxers wasn't that big of a deal.

"What do you want?" I asked, when I recovered the ability to speak. Alona's dire warnings of a vast conspiracy rang in my ears, sounding less and less crazy by the second. Feeling a little foolish suddenly with the lamp above my head, I set it down carefully.

"So suspicious," she said, still frowning.

Now I was getting pissed. "Were you or were you not the person accusing me of ruining your life just a few hours ago?"

She sighed. "You're going to make this difficult, aren't you?" Without waiting for an answer, she reached forward, and I stepped back, the sharp edge of my desk biting into my back, before I realized she was just grabbing for my desk chair.

She rolled the chair toward herself with a smirk that said she'd seen my retreat and found it amusing. She twisted the chair around backward and sat down, her arms resting across the back.

"Where's the queen?" she asked.

It took me a second to realize she meant Alona. "Not here," I said warily. "Why?"

"Good." She nodded.

"What do you want?" I repeated, still not sure how I felt about her being here now. Yes, I was curious. Not sure I was curious enough for a stranger to be in my bedroom late at night when I hadn't invited her.

Alona's voice whispered in my head. *Invasion of your territory; it's a power play.* Damn. Maybe my mom was right. I was spending way too much time with her.

The girl didn't answer right away. She just stared up

at me in that cold, evaluating way that made me feel like I was back in Principal Brewster's office. I took the opportunity to get a better look at her, and though I tried to make it as intimidating and hard a stare as hers, I doubted I succeeded.

She was still wearing her worn-out cargo pants and combat boots. Silver duct tape was wrapped around the toe of one boot, seemingly holding it together. Her dark hair, which I had thought was going to give Alona fits earlier, still stood around her head in a halo, but now it seemed less a result of poor hygiene and more the product of wildly curly hair and possibly being jammed in the hood I could now see at the back of her shirt.

"You know, I had you all wrong," she said finally, using her toes to spin my chair a few inches in one direction and then back, over and over again.

"What does that mean?" I asked, not sure I wanted to know.

She settled herself more comfortably in my chair, as though it were her own. "At first, I thought you were just a curiosity seeker, or some no-talent local out to see what he could see."

Um, ouch?

"Then I thought you were maybe a Casper lover trying to interfere." Her mouth twisted in distaste.

There was that term again. I understood the meaning from the context—and clearly it was meant as an insult— but it was the way she said it, like it was a real thing. Some acknowledged piece of vocabulary I'd somehow missed during SAT prep.

"But"—she leaned closer—"then I had some time to think about it, and you're not any of those things, are you? You don't even know what I'm talking about."

"Well, the no-talent thing was pretty clear," I said.

She grinned and something dangerous gleamed in her eyes, which, I noted with a bit of shock, appeared to be two different colors, blue and green.

"Funny. I like that," she said.

And third time's a charm. . . . "So what do you—"

"I'm proposing an arrangement," she said, choosing her words carefully.

"Uh-huh." Even I could hear the suspicion in my voice.

"You help me out with a little something, and I give you information."

"Information about what?"

She grinned again. "Everything you don't know."

"What makes you think I don't—"

She pulled something small, shiny, and silver from one of her pockets, holding it up and waggling it at me. It was, I was fairly certain, the device that had saved my life by vanquishing Mrs. Ruiz right before my eyes. I could see it had buttons on the top and wires sticking out of one end, details I'd missed before. "Standard issue," she said.

"For who?" I couldn't help myself from asking.

She smirked. She knew she had me then.

Then her expression grew more guarded. "First things

first. You can see them, can't you? I mean, better than I can."
Her mouth tightened as if admitting that last fact had actually pained her.

I assumed she was talking about ghosts. "I don't know. I can—"

"You knew when my aim was off," she said sharply.

Boy, she was not fond of letting me finish a thought. "Yeah, but it wasn't off by that much. . . ."

"When they move, I lose them," she said bitterly. "I can see them just fine while they're still, but when they start moving around, I can't get a bead on them." She shook her head. "It's like my eyes can't keep up with my brain."

That was, oddly enough, something I'd never considered before, when I'd been thinking of the possibility that there would be other ghost-talkers out there. That there would be disparities in level of ability. Though it kind of made sense. Just because a bunch of people could play the trumpet didn't mean they could all play it equally well, with equal aptitude for the high and low notes or whatever.

She looked up at me with a glare, as though daring me to feel sorry for her. "I can hear them better than anyone, though. I heard the princess whining long before I ever saw her." She scowled at me. "How on earth did you end up with that tagalong?"

Somehow I sensed that explaining the whole spirit guide thing might not be a great move right now. "We're friends." Which was more or less the truth.

She raised an eyebrow. "Friends or *friends* friends?"

I wasn't even sure what that meant, but her tone suggested that "*friends* friends" was something more, and not an area I particularly wished to discuss right at this moment because I really didn't know the answer anyway. Alona and I were . . . well, we were just us. That was all.

"What do you want me to do in exchange for this information you're supposedly going to give me?" I asked instead.

She shrugged, looking a little more self-conscious than I'd seen before. "This is my last chance at a containment if I want full membership. I might need a little help getting Mrs. Ruiz in the box." Her voice held a defensive note.

Ignoring, for the moment, that most of what she'd just said sounded like gibberish—"in the box" was a little ominous, and full membership in what?—I had a larger concern. "Mrs. Ruiz? But . . . she's gone. I saw you fire that thing and—"

The girl grinned again, clearly enjoying my ignorance. "Nah, the disruptor just disperses their energy enough to break them up temporarily. It takes multiple hits if you want it to be permanent, and even then, sometimes it doesn't work. On one like her? No way. Did you see the way she was closing those doors on you?"

"I thought she was going to trap me in there with her," I said with a grimace.

She laughed. "She might have. It's been known to happen to a few of us who've fallen asleep at the wheel, so to speak. Not with her, obviously, but other green-levels."

"Green-levels?" I asked.

She just gave me a knowing smile. No more info, not until I agreed to help. Got it.

"So . . . you want my help to get Mrs. Ruiz in the box, whatever that means, and you'll tell me about—"

"Everything," she finished. "Or as much of it as I can. Like I said, I'm not a full member yet."

Of what? I wanted to ask, but I knew better than to try, at least right now. "And then what?"

She frowned. "What do you mean?"

"I mean, you get Mrs. Ruiz and I get all this information, and then what?" I couldn't help but think of Alona's theory that this was some kind of complicated recruiting scheme. "I meet the others or—"

"No," she said sharply. "This has to stay between us."

Oh. "Okay," I said, drawing it out. What was the point, then?

She made an impatient noise and stood, shoving the chair out of the way. "Look, we can help each other here. That's it."

I just looked at her.

She sighed heavily. "If, in a month or two, you want to make contact, I'll show you how to do that. But you and I have never met each other before, get it?"

I nodded.

She stepped closer, grabbing the front of my shirt in her fist. "I'm serious. I know where we keep all the green-levels and worse. Wouldn't keep me up at night to set a few of them loose in your living room, if you can't keep your mouth shut."

I nodded hastily. She was hard-core. I kind of liked that.

She shoved the chair toward me and started for the window, clearly expecting me to follow.

Not without jeans, thanks. "And . . . one more thing," I said. "Your name. Your *real* name."

She faced me and hesitated.

I lifted my hands. I wasn't going anywhere without it. She already knew mine and where to find me. I wasn't completely sure I liked that idea.

"Mina," she said finally. "Mina Blackwell."

I waited.

"Oh, for God's sake," she said in a huff. She reached into the back pocket of her pants, pulled free a battered card, and handed it to me.

It was a driver's license with a picture that showed a slightly younger and much happier Mina Blackwell. She had braces in the photo, which made her look so much more vulnerable. According to the info, she had one blue eye and one green, just as I'd thought, and she was older than me by about six months. "St. Louis?" I asked.

She shrugged. "I go where I'm sent."

"That's a long drive." I handed her back her license.

She tucked it away in her pocket again. "Not nearly as long as if I have to go back without what I came for," she said pointedly.

Okay, got it. Down to business.

* * *

For the second time in twenty-four hours, I ended up hunched in prickly rosebushes at the Gibley Mansion. This time, though, just for a little variety, we were on the opposite side of the former garden.

Most of the cops who'd come roaring in earlier had left by now. Only a couple of squad cars remained at the front of the house. Dopey and a couple of the officers took turns patrolling the inside and the perimeter immediately around the mansion. The rest of the time they stayed out front, making sure their presence was noticeable.

Mina and I were only about five feet from where Alona and I had seen Mrs. Ruiz materialize before. Only this time, instead of facing her, we would be behind her. If she showed up. It felt as if I'd spent days waiting on this ghost already.

Mina's mysterious boxes were back in place, surrounding the exact spot, or close, to where Mrs. Ruiz would appear, the cords trailing directly back to our hiding place and the portable generator, which Mina would leave off until the last second. We were counting on the shadows to hide them well enough until it was time for them to do whatever it was they did. Plus, none of the officers on duty seemed all that interested in the surrounding yard, just keeping people out of and away from the house.

"So, how did you even know about this? About Mrs. Ruiz, I mean?" I whispered to Mina. As long as we kept it down, the officers couldn't hear us all the way at the front, especially over the radios and their own bored gossip. By now, we'd heard enough to learn they figured what had happened earlier was, most likely, a combination of a wild animal trapped in the house and Dopey/Ralph's nerves.

She shrugged, her shoulder rubbing against mine with the movement, and her hair brushing the side of my face. She smelled spicy, like cinnamon and tea or something. Not a bad scent, just different. "Someone on the Decatur Governance and Development Committee called us. Wanted a sweep before the house was destroyed to prevent any future issues. Leadership thought it would be a good opportunity for me to finish up my training." I could hear the sarcasm in her voice in that last part, but I wasn't sure why.

According to what Mina had told me in the car on the way over here, "Leadership" was the ruling body for the Order of the Guardians, a cross between a secret society and a small business, made up entirely of people like us. I'd never even heard of them before, though, and believe me when I say I've done my share of Googling on this topic. In that way, they were more secret society than business, I guess. This thing with Mrs. Ruiz was part of Mina's initiation into full membership. Or full-time work, depending on how you looked at it.

"We do this kind of thing all the time. Clean up after something bad happens in a location, sweep a house before someone new moves in." She shrugged. "Most of the time it's not a green-level, though."

They ranked spirits based on an estimation of their potential to do harm to humans. Like Mrs. Ruiz's ability to slam doors shut. If she could do that, it wouldn't have taken much more to shove someone down the stairs. And based on the history of the house, it seemed she might well have done that, probably more than once.

I couldn't quite resolve this new information with what I believed—to maintain a presence here, a spirit had to focus on the positive rather than the negative. But if that were true without exception, Mrs. Ruiz would have been gone years ago.

Apparently, the system wasn't quite as simple as I'd always assumed it to be. The principle held true, yes, but additional factors figured in, like initial energy level, something I'd never considered. It made sense, though, or else there would be no angry and vengeful ghosts, and I'd met plenty of those over the years.

Evidently, there were also different classifications for the variety of spirits who hung around. Some had no idea that they were dead and frequently relived moments leading up to their own demise. Others, like Alona and Mrs. Ruiz, were fully aware that they were gone . . . and in Mrs. Ruiz's case, less than happy about it.

I hadn't managed to get a complete breakdown from Mina, but I knew that, on a scale, green-levels were closer to the top than the bottom. Hence why she'd been sent here to prove herself.

Knowing that now, I was maybe a little uncomfortable with my role in this test. I was, essentially, helping Mina cheat. Aside from the ethics of it, which I didn't particularly care for, I was also kind of worried that if she "passed," she might end up in a situation she couldn't see well enough to handle on her own.

Trying to bring that up, though, had proven dangerous. She'd said nothing, but glared at me and refused to speak to me, other than to issue more threats if I backed out.

Okay, so I'd learned that lesson. Whatever she gained by full membership, Mina thought it was worth the risk. "How do people even know to ask you guys?" I asked now.

She shrugged. "The people who need to know know. We have a network of contacts among the clergy in all the major religions; state, local, and federal government; hospitals; funeral homes; even some police and fire departments. I think they've even got somebody on one of those paranormal investigation shows."

"Really?"

She snorted. "Just in case one of the 'investigators' actually stumbles into something real, I think."

"And you box all of them? All the ghosts, I mean." *Boxing*, as I understood it, was what she meant by containment. Another part of this I was less than comfortable with. The technology in those boxes—whatever it was, and Mina didn't know other than to say, "Who cares? It works"—would divide up a spirit's energy and prevent it from re-forming. She could then cart the boxes away, and no more haunting. What happened to the ghost after that, she was less clear about. Some of them were studied by the Order's scientists, the same ones who'd created all the hardware she was hauling around. Others . . . she didn't know or wouldn't say.

She looked at me pityingly. "We've been over this. They're not souls. Souls can't be measured or captured. They're shadows, energy echoes, imitations. Whatever."

I wasn't so sure. I understood her point, to an extent. Souls don't register on an electromagnetic scale. But that didn't mean they weren't more than the mindless echoes she was implying.

"If they don't bother the living, we don't bother them," she said. "There are too many of them anyway."

Like they were ants or some other kind of household pest.

"But"—she elbowed me—"we serve the living, not the dead. Remember that."

That certainly explained her attitude toward Alona. I mean, the part that went beyond the attitude almost everyone had toward Alona. She wasn't always easy to like. But that didn't mean I was willing to relegate her to being some kind of . . . nonentity.

Doubt must have shown on my face. "Let me guess. You got into this to help the poor dead people make peace with their unfinished business." Mina sounded amused.

"You don't do that?" I was guessing not. I'd described the white light to her, and she'd readily acknowledged it as a phenomenon she was familiar with. To her understanding, however, it was simply a side effect of an echo willingly surrendering what was left of its energy. What that might mean for Alona, someone who'd been into the light and come back, I had no idea.

"What part of *Vivis servimus non mortuis* do you not understand?" she asked.

"All of it?"

She shifted carefully on the ground next to me, making herself more comfortable, which reminded me viscerally of the last time I'd been in a similar situation with a girl. Suddenly I missed Alona. She would kill me if she found out I was here. And yet, I wasn't ready to walk away. There were still too many things I didn't know.

"Has it not occurred to you that every time you're helping one of them, you might be hurting someone who is still alive?" Mina asked with some exasperation.

"How?" I demanded.

"Shhhh." She elbowed me harder this time, and I grunted.

"First," she said in a quieter voice, "because you're taking one person's—if you can even think of a ghost as anything fully actualized as a whole person—account as the truth."

That danger I knew well enough. I could never know for certain that ghosts seeking closure to their unfinished business were going to be honest with me—or even themselves—about what that business might be.

"Second, even if they are telling the truth, how does it help to let a man know that his dead wife is sorry for something she did thirty years ago that he might not even know about?"

That was, much as I hated to admit it, a good question.

Mina shrugged. "Maybe he's been happier this whole time thinking she's at peace or whatever. And now you're telling him that his wife, or some version of her energy, has been hanging around and miserable, watching him this whole time? No way."

"So, if they're not here because they have unfinished business, why are they here at all?" I felt like the world as I knew it was slipping away little by little.

She made an impatient noise. "You're thinking about this way too much. Why are we here? Why is anyone here?" She shook her head. "It doesn't matter. You just have to look for the greater good."

That, too, made sense.

"Our job is to protect the living. We're the heroes here, not the villains," she added.

The villains in her mind were the Casper lovers. They weren't an organization, at least not like the Order. They were the paranormal equivalent of rabid environmentalists, apparently—people who elevated spirits above the living, almost to the point of worshiping them as deities or emissaries of such, and refused to consider a spirit's departure from this existence a good thing under any circumstances.

I wasn't completely on that side either, obviously. Technically, the Order and I did the same work. I just did it by finding out what was keeping the spirit here and helping him or her move on.

"Speaking of which"—she grinned at me—"I think we have company."

I looked through the tangle of branches and leaves in front of us at the configuration of boxes. I could barely see them in the dark. The moonlight was fading, and the sun would start coming up soon.

A faint glow had started to appear in the open space amid the five boxes, almost directly on top of the dirty pillowcase filled with most of the silverware. Mina had spread the rest of the spoons around inside the circle made by the boxes in an effort to distract Mrs. Ruiz. We were counting on Mrs. Ruiz's obsession with her treasure—no way would she want to lose even one of those spoons—to keep her distracted. Hopefully, trying to pick them up again—for all I knew she might succeed, she was really strong—would keep her so occupied she didn't notice the trap closing around her until it was too late.

This had apparently been Mina's plan before. Lure Mrs. Ruiz into the living room—a location with multiple exits, unlike the bedroom where the silverware had been hidden— and contain her there. Except I'd needed saving first and she'd stepped in. I owed her for that, at least.

Mina tensed next to me. "Ready?" she asked.

My role was simple. Flip the switch on the generator, guide Mina if Mrs. Ruiz tried to move outside the boxes, and then run like hell when it was all done because apparently there was no way the cops would miss seeing the light show that ensued.

No. "Yes," I said.

She nodded, a motion I sensed more than saw in the

dark. She rose into a crouching position. Though I couldn't see it, I knew she'd have the control box in her hand. She'd showed it to me when we unloaded everything from her car. It was a simple device that would trigger the boxes on the ground to open and divide up the energy that was Mrs. Ruiz into five equal parts.

She couldn't do it too soon, before Mrs. Ruiz had fully materialized, or it wouldn't take.

I watched intently, feeling the intensity thrumming through Mina next to me. She was determined to make this work.

The pattern of Mrs. Ruiz's housedress solidified into something resembling real fabric rather than a projection of the same, at about the same time she noticed the spoons on the ground. Or so I assumed. She bent down to try to pick them up, and Mina nudged me.

I snapped the switch on the generator, which started up with what felt like a deafening roar, though that was probably more because it was so close to us and I was dreading getting caught.

Mrs. Ruiz looked up sharply and spun around to face us and the source of the noise, moving quickly for a woman of her size.

"Now," I said to Mina.

She didn't react for a second, and I realized even in the slight movement of Mrs. Ruiz turning around, Mina had lost sight of her. Damn. She really couldn't see them very well.

"Mina . . ."

She pressed the button, and the split tops on the boxes cracked open, sending bolts of yellowish-white light toward the sky.

Oh, hell. There was no way we were getting out of here undetected.

As I watched, the five separate beams converged on Mrs. Ruiz, splitting her into pieces, like a photograph broken apart into sections. Her face was still frozen in that expression of fury.

Then the beams began to retract slowly, each pulling with it the blur of colors that had once been a part of Mrs. Ruiz.

Loud voices came from the front of the house, followed immediately by the sound of car doors opening and running steps.

"Mina," I whispered urgently.

"Wait," she said, her face aglow in the fading beams, intensity and concentration wrinkling her brow.

"Mina!"

She fumbled in her bag and came out with a handful of something. She snapped the something open, and our hiding place glowed green. Glow sticks, but the big professional kind, like for spelunking or whatever. Then she stood and chucked them as hard as she could away from us and our escape path. They spun and arced away from us like mini-UFOs. A couple of them smacked into the side of the house with a loud thwack.

The running footsteps slowed and then stopped. A

flashlight passed over the bushes that hid us and then moved in the direction of the glow sticks.

"Now," she whispered. She pressed another button, and the top of the boxes snapped shut, eliminating the last of glow of the beams.

I snapped off the generator and abandoned it, per plan, and she snagged the cords of the boxes, hauling them over her shoulder.

We bolted through the yard, heading for the street behind the house and the block beyond it, where we'd parked her car, a beat-up Malibu that could have been a twin to my Dodge in all its signs of having lived a rough life.

"Hey!" The first shout came from behind us, and I put on a burst of speed. I did not want to explain this to my mother.

I looked back to see how Mina was doing with the additional burden of her equipment and found her veering away from me.

What the hell?

She must have felt my gaze on her because she paused just long enough to look over her shoulder and give a jaunty salute that I could barely see in the faint light. I started to turn, to go after her, but doubling back would have put me on a direct collision course with all the nice officers chasing us with their flashlights and, likely, guns.

No, thanks.

Damn it. I knew I should have driven myself.

I stuck to the shadows, and instead of heading for the street, as we'd planned, I moved through side yards and backyards of the homes surrounding the Gibley Mansion. Mina, after all, had the keys to her car. Getting to the Malibu would do me no good without those.

Dogs barked, and I tripped repeatedly over garden hoses, kids' toys, and lawn chairs. But I stayed on my feet and kept moving. The historical society apparently forbade fences in this part of town, thank God.

After about six blocks, I had to stop. I bent in half in the side yard of a Victorian monstrosity that had boarded-up windows, trying to breathe without throwing up. The cuts on my back from my earlier encounter with Mrs. Ruiz throbbed and burned.

What was Mina doing?

Leaving you to fend for yourself now that she has what she needed. Duh. The Alona-like voice in my head was dismissive.

I tried to listen for the sound of anyone behind me, but I couldn't hear anything over the pounding of my heart and my panicked panting for air.

Apparently, my arrangement with Mina, what there'd been of it, was now over.

Never trust a mysterious girl who shows up in your room in the middle of the night, no matter how much you may or may not have in common. It seemed a simple—and *obvious*—conclusion now, standing here, alone, in the dark, miles from home.

I waited another long few moments, still catching my breath and trying to pull together my thoughts. The dogs in the neighborhood quieted down, and I didn't hear sirens.

Not this time. Either they'd caught Mina or given up looking for me.

She'd lied about giving me a way to contact the Order. Which, now that I thought about it, only made sense.

The version of Alona in my head made another disdainful noise. *Of course.*

Mina had risked a lot to pass this test, and would she really chance it on me, a stranger, keeping his promise to keep his mouth shut?

Crap. Alona would have seen that coming a mile away. She schemed like this in her sleep . . . or whatever it was she did now.

Hell, for all I knew, Mina had lied about everything, including the existence of the Order. But she belonged, or wanted to belong, to *something*. That much was clear. And her conviction about serving the living and not the dead had certainly seemed genuine enough. Then again, maybe I wasn't the best judge of sincerity at the moment.

Lucky for me, I had one very long walk back to my house to begin sorting out fiction from possible fact.

❧ 6 ❧

Alona

I was used to seeing Will in all sorts of disarray first thing in the morning. Hair standing up, covers in a tangle, arms flopped wide, eyes half-open, and a grumpy expression. Very grumpy, usually. (He is not a morning person. I had never had that luxury in life—zero-hour gym waits for no woman—and didn't now, either. I couldn't have been killed on my way out to lunch?)

This morning, however, was different.

He was laying facedown on the bed, on top of the covers, fully dressed, Chucks still on with fresh grass clippings all over them. In short, nothing like how I'd left him last night.

It was enough to stop me in my tracks, distracting me

momentarily from my goal of getting him up and moving immediately.

"What happened to you?" I asked.

He jumped a little, like the sound of my voice had startled him, and then groaned in response without lifting his head.

"What time is it?" he muttered.

I rolled my eyes, even though he couldn't see me. Like I'd suddenly start showing up at noon. "What time do you think it is?"

He shifted onto his back and raised his hand to block the light coming in the window. "Too early."

I narrowed my eyes at him. *Something* had happened. "Did Liesel come here last night? Because I told her—"

"What? Liesel? No." With an effort, he managed to push himself up into a sitting position. "I'm fine. I just need to wake up."

"You look like you barely slept." I might have taken credit for my exemplary make-out skills, except he'd also been wearing fewer clothes the last time I'd seen him.

His pale blue gaze, bloodshot around the edges, met mine. "It's nothing. Just . . . I heard a noise outside last night."

"So you got dressed to go check it out and forgot to get undressed when you came back in?" I asked in disbelief.

"Something like that." He rubbed his face with his hands.

Wait a minute . . . "Did Erickson stop by?" I demanded. The strain of tuning out spirits for all the years before I'd

96

come along had given Will a couple of bad habits I hadn't been able to break him of yet. The first was his tendency to stick his earbuds in whenever he was being pissy and didn't want to hear what I had to say. The second was his occasional "smoke away your troubles" attitude when his friend Erickson was around, which, thankfully, wasn't all that often. I mean, whatever, but after watching my mother lose herself in the bottle in an attempt to forget, I was a little leery about seeing someone else, who I might also care about a little bit, showing some of the same tendencies every once in a while.

"No, he's in California, remember?" Will stood up slowly, like he ached all over, and shuffled to his closet. Why, I don't know, since half his wardrobe still needed to be put away after its most recent trip through the laundry and stood in piles on his desk, as usual.

I moved around the bed to follow him. "You just seem out of it," I said with a frown.

"I didn't sleep well." He raked a hand through the mostly empty hangers, making a loud, crashing racket. "What's going on?"

I frowned. Something was still not right here, but I could feel time slipping away from me. I'd already lost all of last night, and every minute that passed, more of my life was being pitched to the foot of the driveway in a Hefty bag, and my dad was growing more and more attached to Gigi's replacement spawn.

"I need you to talk to my parents," I said.

He went very still. "What happened? Is everything okay?"

"Yeah, it's fine. They're just being dumb, and I want to remind them I used to exist," was what I intended to say in a very cool, nonchalant voice.

But what came out was, "She threw away my Homecoming Queen sash!" and I could barely squeeze that out over the unexpected lump in my throat. *Crap.* I'd thought I was past the point of being upset about it . . . at least in front of someone else.

Will turned around. "She did what?"

That he took it so seriously (though, it might have been more that he didn't quite understand what I'd said) broke whatever little bit of restraint I had left and tears leaked out . . . again. *Damn it.*

He looked alarmed. "It's okay." He reached out and laid a hand on my shoulder hesitantly. I leaned into his touch, and he wrapped his arms around me.

He smelled faintly of outside, a little of sweat, and something else, almost like cinnamon but not quite. It made my nose itch like a trapped sneeze. Which was annoying, to say the least. But I wasn't about to move away from this unexpected bit of comfort.

"Your mom did this? Threw your sash away?" he asked. I could feel his voice in his chest against my cheek. He was evidently still trying to piece together what I'd said to him.

"Well, it wasn't the whole thing," I said, trying to catch my breath between sobs. "Just this little scrap that I cut off before I had to give it back. No one gets to keep the sash." And now even the bit of it I'd had was gone. A fresh wave of tears started.

"I'm sorry," he murmured, stroking my hair, which felt so good it was almost worth losing some—not all, though—of my treasured possessions. "What else?"

"What else did she throw away? Like, everything that wasn't nailed down."

"No, I mean, did something else happen?"

I pulled back to look up at him with a frown. "Is that not enough?"

"Yes," he answered quickly. "Of course. I just thought—"

"My dad is having a baby." I sniffed. "Not him directly, of course. My step-Mothra."

"Step-Mothra?" he asked, and I could hear the repressed laugh in his voice.

I nodded against his shirt. "Because she swoops in and destroys everything."

He was quiet for a long moment. Then he said, "You do know that in some of the movies Mothra is actually kind of the hero, right?"

I jerked away from him. "*So* not the point."

"Okay, okay." He held up his hands in defense. "You're right."

Slightly mollified, I allowed him to pull me close again and resume that soothing stroking of my hair. "Gigi is her name. My stepmother, I mean. And she's pregnant." The last word escaped like an exhausted sigh.

"I would think that might be a good thing," Will said cautiously.

"You'd think so, maybe, if Gigi wasn't this total bitch, and if you didn't know that my dad always used to tell her he didn't need more kids because he had me. And now he doesn't have me anymore."

"Alona, I'm sure—"

"He took the ultrasound picture and covered up my photo with it." The words came out in a humiliating rush, and I buried my face against his shoulder so there wasn't even a chance of meeting his gaze. I didn't get into the whole thing about how mine was—or used to be—the only photo in his office. It was just too sad and pathetic.

His fingers stopped in my hair. "You know they still love you. They always will, no matter how many rooms they clean out or kids they have."

Yeah, right. He didn't know my parents. "So, you'll talk to them?" I asked.

He stiffened.

"I don't mean you have to talk to them directly." He hated the face-to-face missions. I could be flexible, though. "Just send them a letter or whatever, like we usually—"

"Is your mom drinking again?" he asked quietly.

"What?" I pulled back to look up at him. His expression was too serious. It sent a spike of inexplicable fear through me. "No. Not that I know of."

"And your dad is happy?

"Only because he doesn't know," I argued. "He probably

thinks I'm off learning how to play the harp or relaxing on a cloud or something." We have the most ridiculous ideas of the afterlife.

He let me go and turned to his closet again. But he didn't take anything out, just stared into like it held answers to questions I didn't even know.

"What is your problem?" I demanded. This wasn't anything different than what we did for other people every single day.

"How will it help them?" he asked.

"What?" I asked, certain I'd heard him wrong.

"If they're finally getting to a point where they can move on and—"

"*Finally?* It's only been two months!"

He faced me, his expression tight with frustration. "And what if it makes it worse for them? What if your mom falls off the wagon because she feels guilty about you still being here, or what if your dad decides he can't love this new kid as much because it might hurt your feelings? Then what? How many people end up worse off than they were before?"

I resisted the urge to scream, "So?" because I didn't really want any of those things to happen, but some acknowledgment that I'd been there, that I'd mattered, would have been nice. Instead, it felt like everyone was better off without me. And Will was just not getting it.

"Since when do we even worry about this?" I demanded. "How many letters and phone calls and whatever else have we done without even thinking about the people on the receiving end?"

He flinched. "Maybe we should have," he said.

"No," I said with exaggerated patience. "Our job is not to worry about the living. They can still change things for themselves. It's the rest of us who need help."

"Says who?" he argued. "The light? You can't even tell me for sure what happened while you were gone, can you?"

I gaped at him. "Who are you? Since when do you even think like this? It's like you transformed overnight into some kind of—"

I stopped. Pieces tumbled and clicked in my brain. Will, in bed and happy when I left. Will, dressed and crazy when I came back this morning, and smelling like some kind of nighttime adventure and unfamiliar spicy-girlie scent, and asking questions about my very purpose here, his purpose, our work together.

"Oh." The word escaped involuntarily, more like a rush of air to accompany the socked-in-the-gut sensation I was currently feeling.

His eyes widened, and he knew right then. He knew that I knew.

"You met up with her again, didn't you?" I asked. Just saying the words felt like bleeding.

"It wasn't my fault," he said quickly. "She found me. She came in my window and—"

I shook my head. Of course. *Stupid, Alona.* A total beginner's mistake. I'd underestimated my enemy. I'd thought I wouldn't have to worry about him here at home, just when we were out and about together. She didn't know his name or his address. But it occurred to me now she could have gotten his name from any number of spirits around town. Will was relatively famous, at least among the dead-but-not-quite-gone community. I wasn't used to there being other people around with access to that particular population.

After that, it would just be a simple matter of Googling him on her phone or even going old-school and finding an actual phone book. The Killians were probably listed, and I didn't think there were enough to make it a very long task to find the right one.

I stepped backed from him slowly, not sure what I was going to do, just that I couldn't stand this close to him right now.

"It wasn't like that," he insisted, following me. "She needed my help to box Mrs. Ruiz."

I froze. "Box Mrs. Ruiz?"

Color rose in his pale cheeks. "She wasn't gone. She was too powerful for the disruptor. So we . . . contained her, so she wouldn't hurt anyone again."

"And then?" I asked with a calm I did not feel.

"Then what?"

"And then what did you do with Mrs. Ruiz?"

He grimaced. "Mina took her. The boxes, I mean. The pieces of . . . never mind."

I felt like I was going to be sick.

As someone who'd been knocked around by that

particular spirit, I could fully understand the motivation behind stopping Mrs. Ruiz, but to just give a spirit over to someone he didn't know? Someone who might or might not—and I was leaning toward the latter—share the same concerns about Mrs. Ruiz's fate. Someone who *boxed* her . . . in pieces? Not that she was any great or wonderful person, but I didn't think it was our decision as to who gets to go to the light and who's trapped in some kind of box. How would we know where to draw the line? More importantly, where would he draw it?

And what about me? All that about not wanting to change things, about not wanting to do this with anyone but me?

What if he decided I belonged in a box?

Will stepped toward me, and I backed up immediately, my hands up in front of me, like he might lash out at me. "I don't know you," I said.

He paled. "I didn't . . . she didn't . . . we just talked. She said she could tell me more about people like me. But it turned out she was just using me to locate Mrs. Ruiz. Once she had Ruiz, she left."

But she would be back. Or, he wouldn't stop until he found her. She'd almost guaranteed that just by leaving. I could tell already.

"Now I don't know how much of it was a lie and how much of it was—"

"Wait." I couldn't believe this. "Are you actually expecting me to feel *sorry* for you?"

"She lied, but I don't know—"

"So did you."

"No," he said emphatically, shaking his head. "No, I wasn't trying to change anything. I just wanted to know more about who I am, what I'm supposed to be doing."

"You know what you're supposed to be doing!" Even I could hear the shrill-sounding panic in my voice.

He just looked at me, and through the blurry veil of tears I refused to shed, I could see he wasn't so sure anymore. Whatever she'd said to him last night, it had planted a seed of doubt in his mind. And that was more than enough to ruin everything.

He wasn't going to help me. He might not help any of us anymore. If he had Mina the Magnificent with all her little toys, he wouldn't need to. And he wouldn't need me.

I angled away from him, narrowly avoiding the edge of the desk, searching for the place where that field around him would give out and I could pass through the wall. I needed to get out of here before I started crying.

"Alona," he said. "Please don't."

I ignored him and kept going.

He sighed. "I'm not saying I'm going to stop what we're doing, just that maybe we need to think about it from another perspective."

"The living perspective," I said.

He cleared his throat. "Yeah." His gaze pleaded with me to understand.

Outside, I heard the distinctive rumble-thump of a garbage truck making its rounds in the neighborhood. It was trash day in Groundsboro. If my mother had been motivated enough to drag all those bags down from my room to the curb, my whole life was about to disappear into a landfill forever.

"I just need time to think about all of this," he said.

I nodded fiercely. "I guarantee you're going to have a lot of time to think and a lot more stuff to think about." In less than a day, I'd been crapped on by just about everyone who'd ever claimed to care about me. So, it was going to take a lot more than a heartfelt plea for understanding to change things now, and I wasn't about to wait for whatever that might be. No, I was done with waiting. My afterlife was in my hands now.

"What's that supposed to mean?" he asked, looking alarmed.

He knew me too well. Good.

"It means that since I'm pretty sure I don't meet your definition of 'important,' as in 'living,' it's none of your damn business." Then I turned and walked through the wall.

If nothing else, you have to love being dead for the dramatic exits.

There's always that one thing, right? A particular action that is your own personal line in the sand. The nuclear threat you keep in your back pocket, never even mentioning it because it will escalate any conflict beyond the chance of reconciliation.

And yet, here I was, declaring war, turning that line in the sand into a mere dot in the distance behind me.

The lobby of St. Catherine's Hospital was full of people

during this time of day. Some of them were waiting for appointments with one doctor or another. Others were holding vigils for loved ones on the floors above. My father had walked through this very space on a Monday morning, not all that long ago, demanding information about his daughter and a bus accident.

For not the first time, I wished for a cosmic do-over, a chance to relive that day again. When my dad called that morning, I would have told him to get over it and deal with my mom himself. Then I would have refused to speak to either one until they got their act together. Immature? Possibly, but it would have solved the problem of me being their go-between, which was what caused all of this in the first place.

Well, not this specifically. This—me being here in St. Catherine's, preparing to take last-resort measures—that was all on Will.

He left you no choice, I reminded myself. Even still, I knew he'd never forgive me after this. Whatever "more than friends" vibe had been between us would be gone, dead beyond resuscitation. But my message would be delivered, and he'd know that I didn't need him to do it. That was the important part.

I headed toward the elevators and stood next to a woman with a giant bundle of GET WELL SOON balloons and a huge teddy bear that had one furry arm in a sling. She looked like she would be going to the right place. Now that I'd made up my mind to do this, I didn't want to waste time riding up and down to all the wrong floors.

My hands were sweating. I'd only done this once before and in desperation. What if it didn't work?

I shook my head. No, it had to work.

Though, honestly, the thought of what it would take to succeed almost scared me more than the possibility of failing. Almost.

The elevator signaled its arrival, and I followed the woman and her balloons inside. As I'd hoped, she pushed the button for the fifth floor. Pediatrics.

When the doors opened, revealing the same obnoxious smiley faces and rainbows that I remembered from my first trip, the woman headed off with her bear and balloons to the right. I took a left, past the nurses' desk, acting on the memory of an afternoon I would really have preferred to forget.

As I walked, I counted the doors lining the corridor and stopped when I reached a partially closed one about halfway down the hall. This one seemed right, from what I could recall.

I peeked inside. The room was dim with the blinds mostly drawn and television off, but I could still see well enough to know I was in the right place.

Lily Turner looked much the same as when I'd first seen her a couple of months ago. Not all that surprising, given her permanent comatose state. She lay half elevated in the bed, her shiny light brown hair spread over the pillow behind her. This time, though, at least her eyes were closed. Seeing her staring off at nothing had been creepy as hell.

I stepped inside, passing partially through the door, and couldn't help but notice that while Lily had stayed the same, her room had changed dramatically.

A couple of months ago, she'd had just a few framed photographs here and there. It was like her family had been expecting her to go home . . . or pass on any second.

Now, though, it was like her bedroom at home had been painstakingly brought over piece by piece and reassembled around her hospital bed.

A bedsheet with castles, fairies, and horse-drawn carriages was tacked to one wall, covering up the cinder blocks. Clearly, Lily had not redecorated at home since she was about six.

Books and photo albums were piled up in a sloppy stack on her bedside table. Stuffed animals, well-worn and missing various appendages, guarded the windowsill. Next to them, a ballerina lamp, her pink tutu the shade, gave the room a pale rosy glow.

And then there were the Ouija boards. They were everywhere. It was worse than I'd ever imagined. Will had told me it was bad, but I'd never thought it would be like this. In addition to the old-fashioned wooden board in the bed with Lily, her limp fingers resting on the planchette, a dozen varieties and multiples of each lay scattered around the room. Made of wood, plastic, in bright pink (something wrong with that, for sure) and standard tan and black, old, new, big, small (travel-size Ouija boards?), even a couple that appeared to be made of that weird see-through yellowish material that would probably glow in the dark.

Some were stacked on the floor; others were haphazardly placed around the room, on the nightstand, on the empty bed that would have belonged to her roommate, on the table with wheels they would have used to serve her meals if she could eat that way. Packaging for at least two new boards stuck out of the garbage can, and a stack of unopened Ouija board game boxes rested on one of the visitor's chair.

These boards, I knew, had nothing to do with re-creating Lily's room at home, and everything to do with Will and me.

Last year, Lily had left a party—a first-tier party, one that I'd attended myself—in tears after a confrontation with her "boyfriend," Ben Rogers. Ben was a player, especially when it came to underclassmen like Lily. She really should have known better, but then again, she evidently hadn't had much experience in our social scene. This was all according to Will, who'd been one of Lily's few friends, before she'd tried to gain a few rungs on the social ladder.

In any case, she'd crashed into a tree on her way home from that party and landed herself in the hospital. She wasn't dying, exactly, but she wasn't getting any better either.

Will said her spirit was gone. She'd moved on to the light right away, apparently, but her body had just kept ticking along, at least for the time being.

Then a couple of months ago, Will's other friend, Joonie, had, in effect, kidnapped Lily's body and brought it to Will in the hope that he would be able to find her spirit and put it back in place. Joonie had pieced together Will's secret about being a ghost-talker from his strange behavior and various context clues. She felt Lily's accident was her fault—they'd had a falling out back when the three of them were friends—and she wanted Will to help her make it right. Actually, she'd been beyond *crazed* to make it right. Will had told her that putting Lily's spirit back into her body wasn't possible, but Joonie didn't believe him. Then Joonie's negative energy—fear, frustration, guilt, and regret—in combination with Will's presence and the Ouija board, had manifested itself as a physical force. In frustration with what she saw as his lack of cooperation, Joonie unwittingly targeted Will with that energy. It choked off his air and his ability to breathe, slowly killing him. Joonie had been too caught up in her own misery to see what was really happening. So, I'd done what I had to do to get her attention.

In the heat of the moment, with Will's life in danger, it had been easy. Using the physicality that came from Will being nearby, I'd spelled out the message Joonie needed to hear on the Ouija board and then put my hand inside Lily's to touch Joonie. It had worked. Joonie had stopped; Will had been saved.

But I'd evidently also given Lily's family cause to hope. The quantity and variety of Ouija boards in her room screamed of desperation. *If this one didn't work, maybe another one will. Maybe she doesn't like the plastic ones. Maybe we should get one in her favorite color.* They'd pinned their hopes on every new purchase, never knowing, of course, that there was no perfect board, and even if it existed, Lily wasn't around to use it.

Lily was gone in the only way that mattered. She had moved on to that peace, that blissful space empty of worry and fear, the one I could only remember in the briefest and most frustrating flashes.

But thanks to me, her family thought she was still hanging around, and in fact, I was here today to use that belief to my advantage.

I swallowed hard, looking down at the pale, hospital-thin girl who seemed lost among her bedcovers and pillows. She wasn't exactly pretty, or hadn't been, but she could have been striking, with a little confidence and the right education in hair products and makeup. Now there was also the matter of the jagged scar stretching from her hairline down to edge of her jaw on the left side of her face. But even that seemed to be getting better in small degrees. It looked less puffy and red this time. That part of her was healing, even if nothing else was, and probably gave her family yet another reason to hope.

Could I really do this? Once, I probably wouldn't have hesitated. I'd used people in all kinds of ways when I was alive without thinking twice. My perspective was if you were willing to be used or weak enough to allow it to happen, then you got what you deserved. If you're not a predator, you're prey, you know? But now . . .

One time. That was it. I just needed to get a message across to my parents.

I moved closer to her bed to wait, my heart beating too fast. I half-expected Will to appear in the doorway suddenly and start shouting at me. He knew what I could do. In fact, I was the only spirit he'd ever seen or heard of with this ability. He had to know I'd be thinking of this . . . right?

But Will did not come.

The room stayed quiet and still with only the steady beeping of Lily's heart monitor in the background to break the silence.

Then, a woman with the same light brown hair as Lily's entered the room, bearing a hospital tray with a pathetic-looking sandwich, a wilted salad, and two oranges. Her mother. It had to be. According to Will, her mother rarely, if ever, left Lily's side, hoping she would wake up enough to communicate again.

I watched her approach. She moved like every step was painful. Her hair-ball–brown cardigan seemed three or four sizes too big for her rail-thin frame.

"I brought you oranges, baby," she said softly, like Lily was just dozing and she didn't want to scare her awake. She picked her way carefully around the end of the bed and sat in the visitor's chair on the far side by Lily's head. "I know how much you love them. I thought I'd peel them up here so you could smell them. Maybe have a slice or two if you wake up."

Her voice sounded hoarse with weariness. This woman was giving all she had to her daughter, her every bit of energy, every ounce of strength. If Lily could have been tube-fed the will to live, her mother would have had her up and around in no time.

This was the worst part. To communicate through Lily, I would need someone living to take down my words. I would be using her mother as much as I was using her.

That first time, the consequences of communicating to Joonie through Lily had never occurred to me beyond the immediate benefit—Joonie would stop and Will would live. I hadn't thought about her family, waiting for months on end to see if she would wake up, only to not be around the few short minutes she had appeared to demonstrate some momentary awareness. It must have been devastating . . . and cruel.

It hadn't been intentional, not then. But now it would be, and contrary to what most people, including Will, seemed to believe about me, I did have a conscience. Telling someone she looks like a bloated pumpkin in her new cinnamon minidress (truth) is worlds away from giving somebody's grief-stricken mother false hope (mean).

Just get it over with. You'll do this just once, and then maybe once everything settles down, you can come back and tell her family good-bye for her. She'd probably appreciate that.

I waited until her mother was settled and peeling an orange before I started. I did not want to have to do this twice today. I remembered all too clearly the feeling of losing myself that had gone along with using Lily's body, like we were merging into one person. It had been scary, really scary. And I wasn't eager to experience it again.

I leaned over the side of Lily's bed, lining my hand up with hers. Then I took a deep breath, let it out slowly, and then placed my hand on top of Lily's.

For a second, I didn't think anything would happen. I could feel the warmth of her skin against my palm, but that was all. Then, like I'd broken through the surface tension in a pool, my hand slipped down into hers. At our wrists, the boundary between us smeared, becoming a blur of my still sun-darkened skin and hers, a pale hospital-bleached white.

Trying to ignore the sensation of heat crawling up my arm, even faster than it had the first time, it seemed, I forced my hand forward and Lily's lurched in response. The plastic planchette dug into the wood of the board under the weight of her hand, but I could still move it. It had been easier when Will was here and I could just move the piece around on the board myself, but this would work, too, and it would, I admitted reluctantly, have more of an effect.

MOM

I grimaced. It felt wrong, bad to be using this word for someone who wasn't my mother. Then again, my mother couldn't even be bothered to hang on to my stuff, let alone relocate it somewhere else entirely. She was just trying to survive in the only way she knew how. I got it. But still.

The heart monitor next to Lily's bed picked up a beat or two, but nothing too bad sounding.

MOM

It took a few seconds for Lily's mother to recognize the

sound she was hearing—the scrape of the planchette across the board. She jolted up, the tray slipping from her lap to the floor with a rattle of hard plastic and the crash of ceramic, to stare at the Ouija board on the other side of the bed.

MOM

Ugh. I was sweating already from the effort . . . and I *hate* sweating. The heat from Lily's arm had crawled up my arm and into my shoulder, and a strange pulling sensation had started, like vacuum suction, yanking me downward. The muscles in my back ached with the effort of keeping me upright.

This time, though, Mrs. Turner understood. She paled, raising a shaking hand to her mouth, her gaze fixed on the board, like if she looked away it would vanish.

Okay, what now?

Um . . .

HI

Her mother began this weird laughing, crying thing, with her shoulders shaking and tears streaming, but no sound emerging. She came around to my side of the bed, and she touched Lily's hand. The strange part is, I felt it on *my* hand.

DONT B SAD

IM OK

Her mom nodded wildly, tears flying off her face and splattering our arms and the bed below.

Yeah, I would definitely have to come back and say good-bye on Lily's behalf. I couldn't leave it like this with her mom. She didn't deserve this.

She stroked our arms, and I shivered at the odd sensation. "Baby, I'm so glad you're here. I need you to do me a favor," she said.

Okay, I had not been expecting this.

"Your father needs to see this. Then he'll believe me." She whipped her cell phone out of her sweater pocket and began dialing. "I could record it, but you know your dad, he won't believe anything until he sees it for himself."

So I was just supposed to hang out here until Lily's dad made it in from wherever? I don't think so. I started painstakingly spelling out my message, hoping her mom understood texting abbreviations.

MSG FRM ALONA

"Just wait, please, baby? He needs to see this." Her mother covered the phone with her hand. "You know he doesn't mean anything by it, all that talk about taking you home to . . . to pass. He just doesn't understand."

What?

The strength of whatever was pulling me into Lily gave a great yank, tugging me down until my whole arm was part of her and my chin was melding with her shoulder. And I started to panic.

This force inside Lily's body was slowly pulling me inside. I needed to get out. Now. My message would have to wait until later.

I tried to pull back and found I couldn't even force myself into a standing position.

Crap.

"Jason, she's here! She's doing it right now," Lily's mom said excitedly into the phone. "You need to come see her."

The voice on the other end said something I couldn't hear over the roar of blood in my ears. The weak, light-headed sensation that usually accompanied my vanishing act was now cascading over me. By the strength of it, I was guessing I didn't have much of me left below the knee. The power of my fear was dissolving me where I stood even as Lily's body tightened its grip on what was left.

Lily's mother frowned down at our hand on the board. "Nothing right this second, but she was just doing it," she said into the phone.

The heart monitor in the corner beeped faster and louder now.

"Lily?" Mrs. Turner asked. "Are you still there?"

Calm down. Think happy thoughts. I had to stop the disappearing.

The suffocating heat closed over my face then, drawing me down, filling my nose until I couldn't breathe.

I freaked and lashed out with everything I had left, trying to break free . . . and my fingers, inside Lily's, spasmed. That was it.

I heard the planchette skitter off the smooth wood, and Mrs. Turner gave an anguished cry. The heart monitor shrieked . . . and then nothing.

7

Will

"Are you okay?" Sam, my boss and my mom's semi-boyfriend, stopped by the booth I was cleaning on his way back to the kitchen. "You haven't said much today." He sounded concerned.

"I'm fine." Nothing that about ten hours of sleep and way less frustration in my life wouldn't solve.

I'd chased after Alona when she'd fled this morning, but she was too quick for me, what with me actually having to open doors to get outside. Then I'd driven over to her mother's house, thinking I might catch up with her before she got there, but no such luck. Either she'd gone somewhere else, or she'd gotten there faster than I would have thought possible and was already safely ensconced inside by the time I got there. It wasn't as if I could ring the doorbell and ask for her.

While I was there, I couldn't help but notice the small mountain of black trash bags at the foot of her mother's driveway, lending credence to Alona's story. Ignoring the strange looks from the few neighbors who were out and about, I'd snagged a few bags at random for Alona and tossed them in my trunk. Here was hoping I'd managed to grab something other than a week's worth of her mom's takeout containers or whatever. I hadn't been trying to hurt her this morning. It was just . . . everything was so confusing now.

Then I'd come back home and spent three fruitless, grainy-eyed hours searching on the Internet only to find virtually nothing about any Order of the Guardians—other than a few vague allusions on a conspiracy theory message board—and way too many Blackwells in the St. Louis area.

Now what? I had no idea.

And Alona was furious with me. That couldn't possibly end well. It wasn't like her to be gone for this long, even if she was angry. Especially if she was angry. Her theory when it came to conflict was that it was only effective if the other person was made painfully aware of your perspective— emphasis on "pain"—until he or she had no choice but to surrender. And Alona was all about winning.

But right now, at a little after nine at night, it had been more than twelve hours since I'd seen her last.

"Do you maybe want to move on to a different table then?" Sam asked, drawing my attention back to the conversation at hand.

I looked down to find the once crumb-covered and syrup-sticky table gleaming and shiny wet. The booths on either side of me, which I swore had been full of people just a second ago, were now empty except for the piles of dirty dishes and balled up napkins for me to take away. How long had I been zoned out? I needed caffeine. Immediately. "Right," I said. "Sorry. I just need some more sleep, I guess."

Assuming Alona would let me. I envisioned a mob of angry ghosts gathering at my house—knowing Alona, in my freaking bedroom—right now.

"Well, go home, then." Sam grinned. "You were due to clock out fifteen minutes ago anyway."

"Oh." *Wake up, Will.*

"I'm all for the extra help, but I think your mom'll start getting nervous if you're not home soon," he said.

I nodded. He was right, as usual.

"Also"—he leaned a little closer—"just so you know, table sixteen has been staring holes through you for the last ten minutes." His mouth quirked. "Whatever you did, I hope it was worth it." He patted me on the shoulder and walked away.

For a second, my mind supplied the image of Alona glaring at me from the corner of booth, but I knew that wasn't possible. Well, it was, but Sam wouldn't have been able to see her.

I turned and counted tables until I reached the general vicinity of the teens. I still didn't have the layout memorized, so I wasn't entirely sure which one was sixteen.

Then again, it turned out not to matter because once I was close, I saw exactly who Sam was talking about. Mina. And "staring holes at me" was a polite way of phrasing it. It was more like if she could have set me on fire with a look, she would have done it and gleefully watched me burn.

What the hell? Like she had reason to be angry with me? *That* took nerve.

I dropped my washrag on the table and stalked across the restaurant to her booth.

"Thank God," she said with an irritated sigh as I approached. "I was beginning to think I was going to need to rent a neon sign to get your attention." She was still wearing the clothes I'd seen her in last night, but she looked considerably more rumpled, and the faint stain of a bruise now darkened her left cheek. A half-empty cup of coffee sat on the table in front of her, surrounded by a half dozen empty sweetener packets.

"What are you doing here?" I demanded. "I thought you'd be home, celebrating your success and laughing at the dumbass you left behind to get caught." Me, angry? No, of course not.

"Funny thing about that." She smiled bitterly. "They were watching."

"Who?" I reached for the knot at the back of my apron to take the thing off, so Rosalee, the lead server and technically my supervisor, wouldn't interrupt us to bitch at me for "chatting" during work time. I hadn't clocked out yet, but Rosalee would probably assume I had if I weren't wearing the apron.

"Leadership." Mina nodded tightly. "They said it was for my protection, but now ... now I'm not so sure about that, considering they're far more interested in you than they are in the fact that I cheated." She touched her cheek gingerly with an unhappy sounding laugh.

"I don't understand," I said slowly, and sat down on the opposite side of the table.

"It was a risk, one they couldn't be sure would pay off, but it was only my life, my future at stake." Mina shook her head.

"What are you talking about?"

She leaned forward across the table, her hair skimming the top of her coffee cup. "You should have told me who you were," she hissed.

"I wasn't the one who refused to give a name," I argued back.

She laughed again. "Right. I should have just known. Sorry, but memorizing your family history has never been a top priority."

I stared at her, baffled. Why would my family history be any priority at all? At some point between last night and now, one of us had stopped making sense. I was pretty sure it wasn't me.

She cocked her head to one side. "You really don't know, do you? You didn't have to listen to endless tales of the infamous 'book club'?"

He called it book club, though what kind of book club involves coming back exhausted and all banged up, I have no idea. My mom's words echoed in my head, and I felt a chill.

"What book club?" I asked cautiously.

Mina made a disgusted noise and slapped a business card down on the table. "Be at this address in an hour. They want to meet you, see what you can do. Let them answer your questions."

"Leadership?" I hazarded a guess.

She stood up. "You don't deserve this."

I didn't even know what "this" was, but I sensed arguing with her about it now probably wasn't a good idea.

"You know the thing that would scare the crap out of me, if I were you? If they're willing to go this far to get you, what do you think they'll do to keep you?"

I might have been more worried if I'd understood half of what she was talking about.

"Here." She pulled the disruptor from her pants pocket. "Just remember, this"—she tapped her finger on the open end with the exposed wires jutting out slightly—"is the dangerous end."

She tossed it at me, and I caught it with fumbling fingers.

"And then I guess we'll see if you're worth everything they think you are." She gave me a mocking smile and then walked away.

Well. That didn't sound good.

"Yep, should be fun. Don't wait up." I juggled the phone between my ear and my shoulder and tried to check building numbers as I drove by. This area of town—one of the oldest sections of Decatur—was not the greatest, and the lighting was sketchy at best. This had once been a bustling downtown area and now consisted mainly of empty and papered-over storefronts like blind eyes staring out at me.

"Have fun, sweetie," my mom said. "I'm so glad you're out having a good time. I'll see you in the morning, okay?"

My mother, unused to me having much of a social life, had been astonishingly easy to lie to, something I already felt guilty about. She was so eager for me to have friends that my story of bumping into some buddies from school who wanted to see a late movie didn't raise a single red flag, when it should have hoisted several.

"Okay. Good night." I waited for her response, then closed my phone and chucked it onto the passenger seat.

I could have gone home. I probably should have gone home instead of coming out here on what was probably at best a wild goose chase and at worst some other scheme Mina had cooked up that would get me into trouble.

But there were two things that bothered me about that conversation with Mina that I couldn't quite dismiss: First, how much she really, really did not want me to come down here for whatever meeting this was. Given Mina's previous lack of interest in my health and well-being, I was intrigued by what would cause such concern. In fact, I suspected she was more worried for herself than for me.

Second, could it really just be chance that both my mom and Mina had referenced a book club, one that clearly had nothing to do with reading, in the last twenty-four hours? I doubted it. And what was all that about my "family history"?

I had no idea what that meant, other than something to do with my dad. It was all too much to pin on coincidence. If all of this had something to do with him, I wanted . . . no, needed to know about it.

I squinted at the scrawled address—2600 Lincoln Avenue—on the back of the business card Mina had left for me. The front of the card was simply an 800 number. I hadn't yet attempted to call it, but I might have to if I didn't find the address soon.

I was on Lincoln Avenue already, and the numbers were descending the farther east I headed, so I should have been in the right area. . . .

There. At the corner ahead of me, a huge billboard announced new loft-style condos at 2601 Lincoln Avenue, and directly across the street . . . the boarded up remains of the Archway Theater.

Crap. I braked hard. Fortunately, no one was behind me.

The Archway Theater topped my list of places (along with Ground Zero in New York) to never, ever visit. It was legend.

It had been built in the twenties, before the Great Depression. In theory, it had cultural significance for Decatur as one of the few former stage theaters converted to a movie theater still in existence, though it had been closed for decades. The historical society kept trying to bring it back to life, but people kept getting hurt or dying during the various renovation attempts over the years. Workers fell to their deaths from the old stage, had unforeseen heart attacks, or were electrocuted when the power was supposed to be off.

It was always written off as superstition and coincidence, but in truth, there was something fundamentally wrong with the Archway that any idiot could recognize and no architect or contractor could repair. Back in the twenties, when the plans for the theater were approved, some genius got the idea to build it on some prime abandoned real estate in the center of town . . . right on top of an old hotel that had burned down in the middle of the night a decade before.

Sixty-some people had died in that hotel fire, and some of the bodies had never been recovered. Then, less than ten years later, construction crews started tearing at the ground to build the theater. Not to go all *Poltergeist* on you, but you have to be a special kind of stupid to do something like that.

That kind of mass event, so many violent deaths all at one time in one place, created a unique energy of its own. My guess was that the theater was caught in a reenactment loop of the hotel fire, the same events cycling over and over again and playing out just as they had that night. From what I'd read online, Gettysburg had a couple of big loops like that. Battalions of soldiers still fought for their lives there, even after they'd been dead for more than a century and a half.

Every year, some group of stupid kids dared each other to break in and spend the night on Halloween, and almost all of them came out scared, sometimes hurt pretty badly, and refusing to talk about their experiences.

And yet, here I was.

I shook my head. Why would a bunch of ghost-talkers

want to meet at the most haunted location in town, possibly even the whole state?

Someone honked behind me, and I jumped. I let my foot off the brake and turned down Springfield to get a closer look at the building. The theater sat on the corner with entrances on both sides, though everything looked dark and boarded up tightly. Thankfully. I really had no interest in going inside.

Then as I was driving past, a flash of red caught my attention. A banner, hanging where the old marquee had been, read: NOW UNDER RENOVATION. OPENING SOON!

Great. Well, that explained it. Assuming Mina had been telling the truth at least some of the time last night, this Order organization was involved with the Decatur Governance and Development Committee. I didn't know anything about what that committee did—something about permits or permission or something?—but if someone on it was concerned about "cleaning" the Gibley property before the parking garage was built, then it would make sense that same person might be interested in making sure the theater was equally untainted before opening day.

So maybe they, the mysterious Leadership Mina kept talking about, really were around here somewhere.

I reached the end of the block and pulled a U-turn to double back. This time, I noticed the open lot at the back of the theater, where a building had obviously just been torn down. Amid the still-standing piles of rubble, a half dozen cars were parked haphazardly. But they were all pointed toward the chain-link fence between the empty lot and the back of the theater. And one of them, though it was hard to be certain in the reduced light, I thought might be Mina's beat-up Malibu.

I backed up and pulled into the open lot, gritting my teeth as my poor Dodge rattled and thumped over the uneven ground. I parked next to a pile of bricks, tucked the card Mina had given me into my pocket, grabbed my phone from the passenger seat, and got out.

The sound of my door closing echoed in the surrounding silence. Even the crunch of my shoes on the uneven gravel sounded absurdly loud.

What are you doing, Will? You should not be here. My common sense decided to make an appearance, late as usual.

Just shut up for a second. Let me see if I'm even in the right place.

I made my way through the cars, half-expecting someone to jump out at me, until I reached the one that I thought was Mina's.

I peered in through the window, finding fast-food wrappers and trash on the passenger-side floor, and zombie office-worker dolls glued to her dash, just as I remembered.

It was definitely her car. I was in the right place.

But now what?

"Hello?" I called quietly, and immediately kicked myself for it. Everybody knows that's one sure way to make yourself an easy target. Also, if this were a horror movie and I'd said "Is anyone there?" I'd be dead by now, dragged kicking and screaming under one of the cars by a multiclawed creature of some type.

I supposed I could, in theory, wait right out here. They couldn't leave without their cars, right? But that felt almost disrespectful, like one step short of turning down the invitation to meet them. Not a great tactic to use with people you were hoping to pump for information.

I headed to the fence and found a place where the links had been cut, the freshly exposed metal gleaming in the blindingly bright security light positioned on the roof of the theater.

Holding the fencing aside, I slipped through and onto the theater property. This had probably once been part of the hotel. I'd need to start paying more attention, and not just for signs of people from this world.

The back of the theater didn't look like much, just a short, nondescript building made of crumbling brick with a couple of construction Dumpsters neatly in a row. It certainly did not scream, "Most Haunted Place in the City!"

The security light overhead focused its beam on a door, the only one that wasn't bricked or boarded up. It was a rusty metal with green flaking paint and looked like it would give you tetanus if you just glanced at it, let alone actually touched it. The handle was missing; an open and sharp-looking hole in the metal remained where it had once been.

The door was also open about a foot, and kept that way by a cinder block at the base.

And still, no sign of anyone else around.

Damn. This whole thing smelled of a trap. Or a test. Or something equally unpleasant as either of those two alternatives. Mina had said they'd wanted to meet me, to see what I could do. I was beginning to suspect that this was going to be far less small talk and far more survival of the fittest than I'd anticipated.

Then again, all the people those cars belonged to had to be around here somewhere, right? Maybe they were already inside. They didn't seem much like the coddling sort, again based on Mina's information, so I had a hard time imagining them leaving someone out here just to greet me.

Just turn around, and go home, common sense suggested. *Whatever you find out cannot be worth the living nightmare inside that building.*

And then what? Lose track of them forever? Miss my chance to meet other people like me? Never know if Mina had been talking about my dad?

I wasn't sure I was ready to give up on those potential answers just because I was afraid. I mean, I was right to be afraid. The ghosts inside this building could kill me. They'd killed people who weren't ghost-talkers.

So, it was a risk. A big one.

But maybe that was the point. It was a test. To see if I was worthy. They'd allowed, no, encouraged Mina to take a chance on containing Mrs. Ruiz alone. So, if that were true, then this would not be so out of character for them at all.

I stood there, fifteen feet from the door, trying to weigh my options.

I had Mina's disruptor in my jeans pocket, if I could figure out how to use it. There were several buttons on top, and I hadn't yet figured out the right combination to make the blue beam appear, even though I'd tried a couple of times in the diner parking lot.

I had my cell phone, too. And if things got really bad, I could summon Alona. She would be furious, even more than before, but she'd have no choice but to come when I called. That was the way the system worked.

However, she was not required to help me, and I was guessing, based on her earlier mood, she would not. Plus, who knew how well Mina or any of the others watching might take her arrival?

Still debating, I shifted my weight uneasily, my heart beating too, too fast.

That's when I felt it, this sudden sense of being watched. I looked around, but still saw no one. Not that that necessarily meant anything. There were dozens of places to hide in the shadows, not to mention the fact that every building surrounding the theater was several stories taller, allowing for a variety of easy-viewing positions.

If they'd watched Mina and me at the Gibley Mansion, what was to say that they weren't watching me now?

And even though I couldn't hear a clock ticking, I could almost feel the seconds slipping away. At some point, if I just stood here, my chance would be over before it even began. The door might, literally, close on this opportunity.

This was most definitely a test. And the first step was

just seeing if I'd enter the building.

I started for the door, my knees feeling shaky and some part of me asking over and over again, "Are we really doing this?"

I climbed the two wooden and creaking stairs to the door, and then with just a second of hesitation, stepped around the cinder block and over the threshold.

Immediately, the smell of dust, mold, and rotting wood engulfed me. I grimaced.

It was dim in here, but I could still see pretty well, thanks to the security light outside and the still-open door.

Clearly, this had once been a backstage area for the theater, but it was now covered in piles of discarded plaster chunks, old chairs with the velvet covering rotting away, and splintery and cracked support beams destined for the Dumpster outside. A narrow path cut through the debris, and I could see recent footprints—more than one set— leading the way through the dust.

Ghosts don't leave footprints, not unless they're around someone like me. So, either way, whether these were tracks left by members of the Order or ghosts who'd been given physicality by their presence, this was probably the right way.

I pulled the disruptor from my pocket, hoping I wouldn't have to use it, because I didn't really know how, and started to follow those footprints.

I wish I could say I was surprised when the door slammed shut behind me, leaving me in complete and utter darkness.

I froze for a long second. *Don't panic. Don't panic.*

Easier said than done, though. If I let myself, I could almost feel breath on the back of my neck. I wasn't alone in here, not by a long shot.

I switched the disruptor to my other hand and dug into my pocket for my cell phone. I yanked it out, my fingers fumbling in my hurry. Because it was craptastically old, I had to hold a button down for light. The beep sounded enormously loud in the thick, ear-ringing silence around me, but it did its job, lighting up a tiny area around me and revealing the flashing lack of signal in the upper left corner of its screen. Not surprising, given the age of the building and the thickness of the walls and the general shittiness of my phone.

Now what? Keep going . . . in the dark.

Great.

I started forward again, following footprints that stood out even more in the blue-white light of my cell phone. After just a few steps, the leg of my jeans caught on something in the tight and crowded corridor, and something sharp bit into my shin.

I swallowed back the pain noise. The less attention I drew to myself, the better. If the Archway was caught in a reenactment loop, like all those ghost battalions in Gettysburg (another place on my never-visit list), then the most powerful energies wouldn't stir until the time of night when the hotel had burned. So, if I could stay quiet and get through to where the others were before the worst of it started up again, I might be okay.

My first clue that that might not be possible was the four guys in the suits. In the dim light from my cell phone, it was hard to catch a lot of detail, but I could see ties that were too short and fat to be modern and big heavy-looking leather suitcases at their feet. Definitely ghosts. They were leaning against the left-hand wall, smoking. Actually, only two of them were leaning against the wall; the other two were half *in* the wall—one was only a pair of legs, crossed at the ankle, sticking out of the wall at his knees. He was clearly sitting on a chair, probably one from the long-destroyed lobby. The other one stood facing the others at an angle, almost split in half by the wall running down the center of his body. He didn't seem bothered by it, though. He grinned—his teeth flashing in the darkness—as he nodded at the others in agreement with something one of them had said. Probably the dude in the wall, since I hadn't heard anything.

Creepy as it was, that made sense. The theater to them wasn't real. The lobby of the hotel was, and obviously that wall hadn't been there when they were alive. And unlike Alona, Mrs. Ruiz, and some of the more sentient ghosts, they were trapped in their own time, unaware of anything else. Until, of course, I tried to slip past them, my head down.

"Hey, buddy, you have the time?" one of them called after me.

I paused, hesitating for just a second. If I didn't answer, they might forget they ever saw me. Then again, at least one of them had seen me in the first place, indicating they might not be entirely blind to events and people outside their own ghostly existence.

"Uh, no?" I offered without turning around. It wasn't

true, of course, but if I looked at my cell phone to check the time, who the hell knew what kind of conversation that would provoke?

I heard the sharp tap of his shoes on the old hardwood floor. "You from around here?" He exhaled with the words and smoke swirled past me in a cloud.

I turned slowly. He, the ghost, didn't seem suspicious of me, though he was watching me closely. It struck me as possible that after so many years of reliving their death by fire, some of these ghosts might have started up a hunt for the cause of their death, even if they didn't realize quite what they were doing. If so, good luck to them. Bernard Shaw, a teenage porter, who'd fallen asleep in the baggage room while smoking, had started the fire. *He* had survived, waking up in time to escape with his life. He hadn't bothered to tell anyone about the fire, fearing for his job.

"No, I'm just visiting," I said to the ghost.

"Didn't think so. Not in that getup." He chuckled, nodding at my clothes.

Uh-huh. Right. Okay. "I have to get going. My..." What would make most sense to him? A girlfriend might raise eyebrows if he thought this was a hotel. So might the equally ambiguous "friend" if I seemed too young to him to be wandering around at night. "My dad," I said finally, "is waiting for me."

"He part of the convention?"

His words triggered a vague memory. The reason the hotel had been so full that night was because of a traveling salesmen convention being held in town. Duroluxe Vacuum Cleaners.

"We're just passing through," I said.

He nodded and flicked his cigarette to the ground between us, and I held my breath. This place with all of its dried up wood, rotting velvet chairs, and dust and junk was a fire waiting to happen.

I stepped on the cigarette butt quickly. Fire was one of the most treacherous parts of being a ghost-talker. Being near a ghostly match, cigarette, or, hell, a firework—whatever a spirit had died with—was enough to spark a fire that would cause real-enough damage or death.

"Thanks, kid." He cuffed my shoulder, and I flinched, waiting for him to make the connection that he'd actually touched me, a living person, but he didn't. Then again, to him, for however much longer, until the fire started again, he was a living person, too. After that, everything would be up for grabs.

Once my new friend had walked back toward his buddies, I got going again. Ahead, the corridor opened into a wider area, or so it seemed. All I could really tell was that the light from my cell phone wouldn't reach beyond the edges of the darkness, and I wasn't seeing the piles of junk stacked along the sides that had accompanied my journey so far.

I hurried past the last piles of junk in sight, and out into the open. I could sense the ceiling above me lift in that way you can just feel it when the air shifts around you. I'd moved from a tight and cramped corridor to a larger, more open space. Noise carried differently out here. And the floor beneath me had changed too. Every step I took now thumped hollowly.

Lifting the phone up higher, I caught a glimpse of tattered strands of ghostly white fabric hanging from the ceiling, moving in the draft I'd felt earlier. The top of it, what I could see anyway, was far more intact, still holding a bit of the original rectangular shape.

The screen. I'd made it into the theater. Probably on the old stage. That would explain the hollow sound beneath my feet.

But still no sign of anyone else.

Where were they?

In the distance, at what would probably be the top of the aisle in the seating area, a quick flash of light, like a flashlight quickly doused, caught my eye.

"Hello?" I hurried forward, aiming my cell phone farther out, searching for the stage's edge or maybe even the glint of metal of a not-yet-removed chair in the audience area for an indicator of where the stage might end. There'd be a drop to the floor, not too big, but it wouldn't take much to snap an ankle or . . . a neck.

But taking my attention away from the floor was a mistake. Either they'd already begun renovation on the stage floor itself or they just hadn't gotten around to fixing up the holes where the boards had already given way. One minute, I was moving along just fine, and the next, my left foot caught nothing but air.

My heart lurched into my throat, and I pitched forward,

my hands and then head slamming into the wood still in place on the other side of the hole I'd found.

I clawed at the floor to stop my fall before the rest of me followed my feet and legs.

The disruptor flew forward, skittering out of sight, and my cell phone slipped from my hand, glowing all the way down to the ground beneath the hollowed stage, striking what sounded like metal crossbars.

Shit.

My heartbeat pounded in my ears, and my breath sounded as loud as a scream. The edge of the wood floor, splintery and sharp, dug into the underside of my forearms. My fingertips had caught on the side of a slightly raised board, and now my arms were pinned between the weight of my body and the floor as I hung there in a strained and awkward pull-up position.

The board was flaky and dry beneath my sweating fingertips and my arms were beginning to shake. I wasn't sure which part was going to give first.

I slipped one hand free, feeling my skin tear as I dragged it across the ragged edge, and planted my palm flat on the stage.

With an effort, I forced my shaking and quavering muscles to pull together, and I landed, half on the stage and half in the hole still, panting and breathing in dust and dirt. I could do this. I could make it out.

And then from behind me, a burst of light, the smell of smoke, and dozens of shrieking voices. The Archway Hotel fire had begun.

❧ 8 ❧

Alona

When I woke, a suffocating blackness—the kind of dark your brain rebels against by creating fireworks and faces out of nothing just for something to see—pressed in on me from every side. I couldn't move, couldn't see . . . couldn't breathe.

Stay calm. A good suggestion, but it didn't help with the impossibly tight feeling in my chest and the screaming desire to inhale.

Was this it, the end? The nothingness, nonexistence Will had talked about? I'd had visions of burning pits of flame or watching myself disintegrate like bonfire ash in the wind. Never this darkness and unbearable closeness to something I couldn't even see. I hadn't felt this claustrophobic since I was six, and my dad had accidentally shut me in the closet designated for my mother's dozen or so fur coats, stoles, and wraps. (I'd been playing runway model again, even though I'd gotten in trouble for it the week before. Hence the hiding in the closet with the furs instead of dragging them out and down to the front hall, which any reasonable person could see cried out for runway use. It had been like being trapped in an animal . . . one that was inside out.)

But the weird part about this, aside from unending darkness, was I was still me. Didn't oblivion—as Will had described it—mean I wasn't supposed to exist? Like maybe your name and the memory of your life was always right there on the edge of your awareness, but you couldn't quite recall it . . . forever.

Unless remembering was the point. I would know there was an existence other than this, and that was my punishment. To be stuck here, knowing what I could never have again, trapped in this unrelenting darkness forever . . .

No. Something about this didn't seem right, and not just in the gigantically, cosmically unfair kind of way. Whenever I'd vanished before, lost control and let the negative energy wash me away, I had no memory of it. I didn't exist during those times. They were just blanks. Like a night at a really bad party.

This, though, was different. I was here. Wherever here was.

I struggled to concentrate, trying to ignore the feeling that my lungs were about to burst. The last thing I remembered was . . .

It took a second for the memory to surface and then fall into place.

I'd been in Lily's hospital room, borrowing her hand to deliver my message, but something had gone wrong. The force connecting my hand to hers had grown more powerful and started to pull me down. And I, unpleasant as it was to admit, had freaked out, caught between the unknown power tugging at me and my own fear and anger, which had slowly begun to consume me.

So, if this wasn't the final nothingness, which seemed unlikely as I was still here and aware, unlike my other temporary bouts of nonexistence, then that left really only one other option . . .

Oh, no. No, no, no. If I could have shaken my head violently in refusal, I would have. This could not be. It would just be wrong, on so many levels.

But, my brain insisted, it made sense, on the surface at least. I'd felt the strength of the connection the very first time I'd used Lily's hand to touch Joonie. Whatever it was, it had not wanted to let me go, and that was only after a few seconds. This time it had been stronger and even more reluctant to release me. Add to that the utter darkness and silence around me and the sense of being completely enclosed, and I had to at least consider the possibility . . .

There was a good chance I'd been pulled *inside* the body of Lily Turner.

I gagged just thinking about it. Me, trapped in someone else's body. How did that work? Was it even possible? No, never mind, I didn't care. If that's where I was, I needed out. NOW.

I started to panic, and my breathing, or attempts at it, sped up. I lashed out with my hands and feet, feeling the effort of my would-be limbs, straining against the press of my lightless surroundings. The darkness gave a little with my increasingly frantic motions, but it didn't retreat. It covered my mouth and nose, pulling in closer with my every frantic attempt at inhaling. It was like trying to breathe with one of those big black garbage bags pulled tight over my face.

Stop it. Calm down! I forced myself to be still, though every moment of doing nothing felt like a slowly dying eternity. *Think, Alona.*

You can do this, I told myself, trying to sound as calm and reassuring as possible. *You got in here. You can get out.*

Except I wasn't entirely certain I'd been the one who'd gotten myself in here. Something had pulled me down. Would that same something let me up?

All right. I forced myself to calm down and slow my breathing. *Let's just think this—*

A bolt of invisible lightning slammed into me, ripping away what little breath I'd gained. Agony poured through me. My back arched, and I twisted against the surface of whatever held me in place, my mouth open in a silent scream.

Okay, okay! I'm sorry. I didn't mean to—

A second bolt, equally stealthy as the first, struck, paralyzing me in another endless wave of pain, crackling along nerve endings that shouldn't have existed. How could something hurt so badly when I didn't have even the semblance of a body, let alone a real one?

I sagged in place, unable to move away, unable to fight, forced to simply wait for the next inevitable blast to tear through whatever remained of me.

Seconds—though it could have been hours for all I know—ticked by, a longer gap than had transpired between the first and second bolts, and nothing happened.

Maybe ... maybe that was it. Maybe it had just been the two—

I'd no sooner let my guard down to begin that thought before the lightning returned, even more powerful than before.

Only this time, something was different. In the silence that followed—I couldn't even breathe through the pain; it was worse even than that time I got sunburned and exfoliated way too soon—I heard something I'd missed before.

Voices.

They were muffled beyond recognition or even understanding, but voices nonetheless.

Someone was out there. Multiple someones, it sounded like. But as the effects of the lightning receded, so did the voices, until I was left in the silent blackness I'd awakened to, however long ago.

But now I knew. I was ready.

When that fourth bolt struck, I didn't fight it. Fighting did no good anyway. I let it roll through me, doing my best to imagine it passing through the body I used to have and still saw in my mind's eye.

And I reached for those voices.

My first clues that something was happening were subtle. The shading of the black around me shifted to a lighter, fuzzier gray. I had more room to breathe. A sudden rhythmic booming filled the air. My heartbeat? It was way too loud.

The voices grew louder and more distinct, and I followed them, intent on escape. Where there were voices, there were other people. People NOT trapped in someone else's body.

"Give me three-fifty."

"Wait! We've got a rhythm."

"BP is eighty over sixty."

"Push another twenty cc's."

The voices spoke over one another, and equipment clattered loudly. A woman sobbed somewhere nearby.

"She's stabilizing."

Wait. This all sounded very familiar. Too familiar. It was hospital-speak. The same I'd heard when I'd watched them try to save me, save my body, rather, that day after the school bus. Only that time, there'd been no stabilizing. No rhythm. No relief in the taut voices, as there was now.

They were saving my life. No, not mine. Lily's?

I needed to get out of here right now. If she was dying, I didn't want to get stuck in here.

I pushed my way through the remaining layers of gray and surfaced—finally!—in a pool of light far too bright.

I threw my hand up to cover my already closed eyes . . .

or rather, I tried. I felt a finger or two twitch, but no real movement. My arm felt heavy and too . . . fleshy. Like I'd suddenly gained hundreds of pounds.

You're just weak, I told myself.

But something didn't seem quite right about that.

My whole body ached, like I'd been locked in the same position for days. Like when you wake up after sleeping twelve hours without moving. My whole left side, but particularly my left leg, felt . . . off in some way. My head throbbed with a ferocity I'd never experienced. And I could feel hands poking and prodding at me, removing medical equipment, checking my pulse.

No, no, no. This wasn't right.

With my heart pounding too fast—and a beeping somewhere nearby that seemed to keep time with it—I forced my eyes to open a slit and to stay open, despite the light, which made them water fiercely. I couldn't move my head at all, but even that tiny slice of vision, blurry and painful as it was, was enough.

I stared at the girlie pink bedsheet, with castles and fairies hanging on the wall opposite of where I lay. I'd seen it before, but never from this perspective, from the point of view of the one for whom it had been hung. Arms that weren't mine—too pale for one and too freckled for another—rested at my sides. The rise in the blankets farther down that had to be feet and toes was far too close, and yet, when I concentrated with the intensity I'd once reserved for landing a backflip, those toes moved. Just a little, probably not even noticeable to anyone else. But it was enough, more than enough.

I had not escaped Lily Turner's body after all. No, instead, I'd somehow just managed to lock myself into the driver's seat.

Okay, so the important thing was not to panic. Right. I was only stuck inside of someone else's freaking body! And not even one I would have picked for myself, BTW.

Just stay calm. My eyes snapped shut again, and I allowed it, the burden of keeping them open too much in this moment.

It had been one thing to sort of borrow her hand. I'd been aware of my hand inside of hers, like a hand in glove, if you'll excuse the grossness of the metaphor (don't think about it too hard). But this was different. I no longer had any sense of me *within* her. It was just all blended and blurred together. *We* were blended and blurred together.

That couldn't be good. The monitor next to me beeped a little louder and faster, sounding my panic for me.

And apparently, I wasn't the only one having trouble with not freaking out. As soon as someone pushed the rattling cart of equipment away and the doctor left with murmured words that I could not quite hear, the chair next to my bedside squeaked loudly as someone collapsed into it and began to sob.

Lily's mom. It had to be.

Her warm fingers wrapped around mine, startling me,

and she squeezed almost too hard. "Come on, baby, you can't give up on me now."

The anguish in her voice ate at me. I'd caused this. Even if I wasn't sure how, my attempt to use her daughter had brought this about. God, I was a sucky person. Not that it was entirely my fault. Will had some responsibility in all of this. If he'd just done what he was supposed to—i.e., what I said—none of this would have happened!

I wanted to pull my hand away from Mrs. Turner, but succeeded in only wiggling my fingers.

She drew in a breath sharply, and I could feel her staring down at me. "You want your board back, baby?"

Crap. This monster was all mine . . . and Will's.

Will. He might be able to fix this.

Yeah. He could probably just reach in and pull me out. Or, better yet, just "call" me from someplace farther away and I'd have to come out to answer. That's the way it worked. I couldn't ignore his call. Period. Ever. And trust me, I'd tried.

So . . . all I had to do was get Will here. I could do that. It was possible that maybe I'd be pulled out of here tomorrow morning anyway and show up at his side, just like usual. Possible. But I wasn't willing to take the chance. Plus, I was not cool with spending one second longer in this body than I had to, let alone the hours that still had to pass before 7:03 a.m. would roll around again.

"Can you call Will Killian, please?" is what I imagined myself saying in a voice creaky with disuse.

Instead what came out was ... nothing. My throat worked, and my tongue clicked and clacked against the roof of my mouth, but not so much as a grunt emerged.

What the hell? I was stuck in here without any control or a voice? A shiver of fear ran over me and I *felt* it in a way that I hadn't in a while, with real goose bumps and everything. It was almost too intense.

"Let me get your board." She gave my fingers one last squeeze and let go.

I squinted again, and this time, the light wasn't as unbearable. Don't get me wrong, it was still like staring directly at the sun in terms of pain, but I was beginning to adjust. If I avoided looking directly up—at what I was beginning to suspect were ordinary room fluorescents, too bright for my newly sensitized eyes—I could see a bit more.

Straining my eyes to the right, I watched Lily's mom turn away from me and fumble through the stack of Ouija boards on my bedside table.

But before she could put one in place and I could test my likely nonexistent fine motor skills, running footsteps sounded in the hall, out of place now without alarms sounding or the announcement of code blue on the overhead.

They came to a stop right outside my door. Lily's mom froze, her arms wrapped around a pink plastic version of the Ouija board. She jerked around in her chair, and I struggled to follow with my limited range of vision.

"What happened?" A ragged male voice asked from the door. "Is everything okay? Is she—"

"What are you doing here?" Mrs. Turner stood and turned to face him, blocking my view. "I didn't call you."

A too-long pause followed. "I asked the nurses to leave a note in her chart to call my cell phone if she—"

"What, died?" Mrs. Turner spat. "Disappointed, Jason?"

"That's not fair! She's my daughter, too."

"Really?" She moved toward the door, out of my range of vision. "Then where were you this morning? When she was present and trying to communicate?"

He sighed. "Corrine, she's not ..." He took a deep breath. "Never mind. What happened?"

Mrs. Turner sniffed. "Her heart stopped. All of a sudden. No warning."

"She looks different," someone else said, also near the door. God, could everybody please move into the room so I could have a shot at telling what was going on?

This new voice had that squeaky sort of braying quality that I'd noticed in the freshman boys who'd attempted to talk to me. Lily's younger brother?

"He should not be here," Mrs. Turner hissed. "He doesn't have to see this."

"It's his sister," Mr. Turner, presumably, hissed back in that way parents have of arguing in front of their children. Seriously. Do they think we're that stupid? Of course, my parents had graduated from loud, angry whispers to shouting, and then, even worse, stony silence, a long time ago, so this was nothing new to me.

It didn't seem to faze Lily's brother either. He left them

hissing and snarling at each other near the doorway and came closer to me, his shoes squeaking on the floor as he approached.

He stepped into my field of vision, keeping a cautious distance from the side of my bed, but still close enough for me to get a good look.

God, geekiness must run in their family. He was twelve, or maybe thirteen, and tall and skinny with fine light brown hair that was sticking up in the world's worst cowlick at the back of his head. He was wearing a polo shirt (points), but it was about three sizes too big and in a spectacularly bright shade of clearance bin yellow. Seriously. Did they not have a mirror in their house? From this and what I recalled from the pictures I'd seen of Lily, you wouldn't think so.

He stepped a little closer, frowning. Behind him, his parents continued arguing in fierce but hushed tones.

"Corrine, you heard them. Even if she woke up, which is never going to happen, she won't be the same person."

"Not in here, not in front of her," she snapped.

The brother waved his hand millimeters above my face, releasing the smell of antibacterial soap and sweaty boy, and I blinked in irritation.

He cocked his head to one side. "You should see this. She's opening and closing her eyes."

"It's just a reflex, Tyler." Lily's mother sounded exhausted. "Remember, they explained that."

He stared down at me with a frown. "No," he said. "This is different." He rested his hands on the side of my bed and leaned in for a closer look. Having him hanging over my face was, quite frankly, more than a little annoying, but it was further than I'd gotten with Mrs. Turner.

Now just get them to give me one of those damn boards. I tried to tell him with my eyes. That would be a start at least. Even if I couldn't quite get it right from the start, maybe they'd at least realize I was trying.

But his parents ignored him.

"I think it's time to take her home," Mr. Turner said.

That sounded like a good plan to me. If "Lily" came home, Will would have to come visit. Guaranteed.

"Take her home to die, you mean," Mrs. Turner said scornfully.

Wait, what?

"Yes, to die," he said. "She's not getting any better. And you're . . ." he sighed. "This isn't good for you."

"*Don't* pretend to care about Lily or me."

I wished I could see her. Mrs. Turner sounded like she was inches from snapping and throwing a punch. From what I'd seen of her, I bet she could probably put some force behind it, too.

"You're willing to let her slip away just so you don't have to live with your mistake," she said.

"That's not—"

"You gave her the car!"

This sudden shout from Mrs. Turner was a conversation stopper. Even Tyler half-turned from me to stare at his parents.

"Yes," he said without hesitation. "I gave our sixteen-year-old sober and responsible daughter the car keys and permission to spend time with her friends. You would have done the same thing, but I'm the one who will have to carry the knowledge for the rest of my life that I could have done something." His voice cracked. "I could have stopped her, but I didn't know." The sound of broken and hoarse breathing, half-repressed sobs came from his direction.

I turned toward the sound instinctively and found I could move my head on the pillow. Just a little bit. But enough to see them both now. Mr. Turner was this big guy with a beard, but his voice was gentle. And I'd forgive him for wearing a denim shirt. He was clearly grieving.

"I'm sorry," Mrs. Turner said wearily. "I didn't mean it." She rested her head against his shoulder, and he allowed it, patting her back with one giant bear-paw of a hand.

"If we take her home," Mr. Turner continued, forcing himself to talk through his tears, "she can be comfortable. She can be with us. No more tests, no more feeding tubes, no more doctors."

Mrs. Turner leaned into him and shook her head. "I don't know. . . . She was trying to talk to me, Jason, I know it."

"Then why don't any of the tests show improvement? Why doesn't she communicate when we ask her to?"

"I don't know, but—"

"Her fingers move on their own—muscle reactions. If you look hard enough, you can make meaning out of anything."

"She told me not to be sad."

"How much of that is what you wanted to see?" he asked gently. "How sure are you that she was reaching for the 's' and not the 't' or the 'q'?"

I beg your pardon, I hit those letters with precision. Well, as much precision as I could manage using someone else's hand.

"I know what I saw," Mrs. Turner said, but her voice had lost its earlier conviction.

"We don't have to forget, we never forget, but she can let go and so can we," he said quietly.

And take me with her? I don't think so. I still wasn't sure how I'd been pulled in here in the first place. If Lily died, would her body let me go? I could think of one thing way worse than being stuck in a living body I didn't want, and that was being stuck in a not-living one.

I shuddered on the inside.

Lily's brother was still by my bed, half sitting, half leaning against the edge, like he'd forgotten I was there in the drama created by his parents. Couldn't blame him. I wasn't exactly the chatty type these days, now was I?

This time, I didn't even try to talk.

If I was going to stop them from letting Lily die long enough to let me out, I needed to let them know I was in here. I seemed to be having better luck with small motions over talking, and the brother's hand was resting on the bed, just inches from mine. If I could just tap him, that might be enough to get his attention and get him to make his parents *see.*

I focused all my effort on my right hand. I just need to move the fingers a little farther down and . . .

As usual, when I really put my mind to something, I win. Big time.

I watched as my hand shot forward and locked around Tyler's wrist.

Tyler jumped up with a yelp, but my hand was still on his arm, so he dragged me with him until I was listing awkwardly to the side.

"Lily!" Mrs. Turner shrieked.

She shoved Mr. Turner away and bolted for the bed. Pushing past Tyler and breaking my now weakening grip on his wrist, she scooped my upper half up into a too-tight hug.

"I *knew* you would come back. I *knew* there was a reason to keep hoping," she whispered in my ear, her tears wet against my face.

Crap. This was going to get complicated.

9

Will

The smoke grew thick quickly. Choking on it, I dragged myself the rest of the way out of the hole, praying the rotten boards would still hold my weight.

Then again, the air beneath the stage was probably cleaner. Ghost smoke seemed to follow the same rules as the real stuff. The trouble would be surviving the fall.

Though my lungs were screaming at me to rest and catch a breath of clean air that would never come, I forced myself to crawl across the rough and ragged boards, staying low where the smoke was the thinnest. Splinters from the rotting boards tore into my palms, feeling more like insect stings, but I kept going.

Flickering light, like what I remembered from burning

leaves in the fall, lit up the theater around me in a manner anything but soothing or nostalgic. I could now see out into the audience area, the rows of seats still in place and the gaping holes where some had already been removed. Through the smoke, I caught a glimpse of double doors, sagging on their hinges, at the top of the main aisle. That was where I'd seen that flash of light. That was where I needed to go. There had to be another way out of this building.

Behind me, a shriek of agony filled the air, so loud and piercing it stopped me in my tracks.

I jerked my head around to see something vaguely person-shaped, covered in writhing flames. Two arms waving in the air, two legs stumbling forward, all of it haloed in bright yellow-and-orange fire. A dark gaping hole in the blaze that encompassed the head might have been the mouth.

Move, Will, move! I scrambled toward the edge of the stage.

The burning man followed me, lighting up the darkness as he moved. His screams were no longer even recognizably human. If I survived this, I'd never be able to go to sleep again without hearing those sounds in my head.

Frantic to get away, I half slid, half fell off the edge of the stage, landing hard and awkwardly in the debris. Above me, the burning man loomed, inches from falling and landing on top of me.

I scrambled backward, hands and feet scrabbling for purchase.

My fingers brushed the smooth edge of something that

did not feel like decaying wood, a disintegrating chunk of plaster, or rusty metal.

The disruptor. It had gone over the edge before me.

I fumbled for it, praying I was right. It took me a couple of tries to get my shaking hand around it. Yes, definitely the disruptor. I could see the gleam of the rough metal edges in the firelight.

The burning man above me wobbled, wavering on the edge.

I closed my hands around the disruptor, turning what I hoped was the open end away from me and started pressing buttons in desperation.

But nothing happened, and the man on fire tipped over the edge of the stage, falling toward me. I shut my eyes and threw myself backward, but I knew it wouldn't be quite enough. The entire pile of debris would be up in flames in seconds and me along with it.

Alona. What would happen to her if I—

Then, behind my closed lids, I saw a burst of blue light. I opened my eyes to find a beam of light coming from somewhere behind me. It had caught the burning ghost in midfall and now held him in place just a foot or so above me.

The man was still covered in flames, but they no longer moved and writhed over what remained of his skin.

Against my will, my mind picked out features of the ghost's mangled face. What was probably his nose, where his eyes had been . . .

Then he disappeared with a faint pop.

I sagged back on the floor, aware suddenly of a sharp pain in my side and an ominous-feeling trickle of warmth.

"Move in," a man's voice barked from behind me.

A rush of fresh air flooded over me. Dark figures, maybe a half dozen or so, moved past me swiftly, little more than shadows. I watched as they leaped onto the stage with ease, their faces disfigured and odd in the shadows of the dancing flames. They alternately wielded fire extinguishers and disruptors, coating everything with explosions of white foam and blue light. Members of the Order. Finally. Apparently I only needed to *almost die* for them to show themselves.

"Are you all right?" someone shouted.

I sat up gingerly and looked back to find two men and a woman hurrying down the aisle toward me. The one closest to me, a dark-haired man in a flannel shirt, jeans, and worn work boots, looked sort of familiar. The woman behind him appeared to be in her late thirties and looked like a Barbie doll come to life, all blond hair and boobs in a tight leopard skin shirt. Not, mind you, that I was complaining. She moved along as best she could in a skirt that cut her steps in half. The last of the three was an older, white-haired guy in a full three-piece suit. Portly might have been a kind description.

Beach ball in clothes would be more accurate, I could almost hear Alona saying.

Was this possibly the almighty Leadership Mina kept going on and on about? They didn't look like people in charge of a secret organization. They looked like part of the happy hour crowd at Buffalo Wild Wings.

The first man knelt next to me and held out something. A clear mask, attached to a metal bottle.

"Put it on." He nodded at it. "You need the air."

I could hear the air hissing out of the mask, clean oxygen that I could almost smell simply by the absence of smoke, dust, and everything else. I fumbled for the mask and held it against my face.

"Why didn't you use the disruptor, boy? That's why we have them," the older man in the suit demanded, panting. He bent in half, hands on his knees, trying to catch his breath.

"You doing okay there, Silas?" the woman asked. She smiled at me, seemingly undisturbed by the chaos around her, other than occasionally batting away bits of ash before they could reach her hair.

Silas, the portly suit guy, nodded.

"He tried to use it," the first man answered for me grimly. "He didn't know how."

The other two looked at me for confirmation, and I nodded, more than content to save speaking for later and concentrate on just breathing for now.

"Mina!" the man in flannel bellowed toward the stage. Uh-oh.

I turned in time to see one of the figures on stage break off and head toward us . . . slowly. She drew the mask off and draped it over her shoulder as she reached the edge of the stage, staring down at all of us defiantly.

"Did I not make it clear what your assignment was this evening?" His tone was cold enough to send a chill through me.

Mina shifted her weight uneasily. "Yes."

"You gave him the disruptor, but you didn't show him how to use it."

"He didn't ask," she snapped. "And isn't that the first rule, never take a weapon you don't know how to use? That's what you always say."

"You didn't even give me a chance," I argued, my voice muffled through the mask.

"It doesn't matter." She threw me a bitter look. "I knew they would save you. Can't risk losing this one."

"That daughter of yours is out of control, John," Silas said with clear disapproval.

Daughter? Well, that would explain why he looked sort of familiar. Now, looking back and forth between the two of them facing off, I could see further resemblances. The same stubborn set to the chin; the way they both squared their shoulders.

"Mina, wait for me outside. We will discuss this later," John said.

She flinched, more a hunching of her whole body, actually, and then she turned away and walked back across the stage. All of sudden I started wondering about the bruise I'd noticed on her face earlier.

"I apologize for my daughter. I sent her to talk to you because I thought she would be a familiar face, at least,"

John said. "I didn't realize her personal concerns would interfere." He grimaced.

"All the more reason the boy should come with me for training," Silas said quickly.

"Excuse me." The Barbie woman put her hands on her hips.

"Now, don't get your panties all up in a bunch, Lucy," Silas said. "I'm just saying the—"

"He lives here. He should, by regulation, train with the Central Division," John said.

"Yes, because your offspring has succeeded so wildly under your supervision," Silas snapped.

I pulled the mask off. "Hey."

They continued bickering.

"Hey! I'm right here." I forced myself to stand up. Nothing felt broken, but I could feel a long scrape on my side even without looking. "I'm not going anywhere with anyone. I came here tonight for answers."

The three of them turned to me surprised, and I waited for the outburst, for someone to lecture or shame me for interrupting.

Instead, Lucy burst into tears. "I'm sorry," she said, flapping her hands at her face like she needed to cool down. "You just sound so much like your father."

I froze. "My dad?"

Lucy didn't answer. She just tottered down the aisle in her crazy-high heels and gathered me up in a warm, very bosomy hug.

"We didn't know, not until now," she said in my ear. "Danny registered you as a null a long time ago. Why would he do that? Why?"

So it wasn't just that my dad hadn't told me about the Order. He hadn't told the Order about me, either. I mean, obviously they'd been aware of my existence, but not that I had ghost-talking abilities. Why would he hide that from them? Why would he keep me from people who could help? None of this made any sense.

I untangled myself from Lucy's arms carefully and stepped back. "I think somebody needs to start at the beginning."

So, it turns out the Order of the Guardians is divided into three sections geographically: Western, Central, and Eastern. They followed the time zone lines roughly, with Western and Central divvying up the states in the middle that would have been the Mountain region.

A leader is appointed to each division by a convoluted election process I still didn't understand even after Silas, Lucy, and John had each taken a crack at explaining it to me.

Each leader was responsible for managing the requests for help and services that came in through the 800 number for his or her appointed region, funneling them out to the members who worked for him or her. Occasionally, cross-regional cooperation was required, as in the development of new technology, a location with a severe haunting, or the certification test for a new full member. But for the most part, Silas took care of the East, Lucy the West, and John everything in the middle.

But the most interesting and shocking part in all of this bureaucratic info was simply this: John Blackwell's predecessor, the previous leader for the Central Division, was none other than my father, Daniel Killian.

"I don't understand. He never said anything." I sat down heavily in one of the discarded chairs, ignoring the plume of dust that resulted.

We were in the lobby now, away from the last of the smoke and flames while the rest of the members that Lucy, John, and Silas had brought with them finished up. I'd seen lots and lots of those little metal boxes going in and couldn't decide how I felt about that.

The three of them exchanged a glance, and then John finally spoke up. "Danny and I trained together. It was always harder for him because his mother, your grandmother, didn't agree with his choice."

"To serve the living," Lucy spoke up.

"She didn't understand the importance of what we do. She preferred to play at helping the echoes." John made a face, as he paced back and forth in front of me.

Helping the echoes? Oh, the dead, ghosts. That would make sense with the story my mom had told me about my grandmother giving her a message from my mother's grandmother. A member of the Order would probably never have done that.

"He was conflicted. It wasn't his fault," Lucy protested.

"He couldn't see the good we were doing except as harm to the ghosts, and vice versa," she said to me.

"He started to pull back from his responsibilities a long time ago, right after you were born, but he didn't actually resign until about five years ago," John said.

"What about the 'book club'?" I asked.

John looked startled. "You remember that?"

"No, it was something my mom said."

He grimaced. "Danny didn't want anyone else to know what we were doing on the weekends when we worked for the Order, so he started calling it that. Became like an inside joke, I guess."

"We tried to talk him out of leaving," Lucy said, pleading with me to understand. "And then he just . . ."

"Killed himself," I said.

John and Lucy flinched.

"All of that is in the past. His choices don't have to be yours," Silas said shortly, stuffing his hands in his pockets.

"We could really use someone with your skills. We saw you interacting with them. It's a smart move when you're outnumbered," Lucy said hopefully. She rolled her flashlight between her palms, making the light spin crazily on the ceiling.

"You had to save me in the end," I pointed out.

"Training," John said with a dismissive wave.

"Yes, training," Silas said with a different emphasis on it. "As in, he needs it. Lots of it."

"But you have the inherent ability to see them, track

them, we could tell that," Lucy said eagerly. "That's rare, especially without the years of intense practice. You could be a full member in a matter of months."

The silence held for a long moment, her hopeful words still hanging in the air.

"So what does that mean?" I asked finally. "What do you want from me?" My head was spinning, but not so much that I missed the distinct undercurrent of tension in the room. There was an endgame here, even if I wasn't sure what it was.

"Undergo formal training, see if you can officially become one of us," Silas said with a shrug.

"If?" Lucy scoffed at him.

"If he stays in the Central Division," John said, "he can continue to live at home and—"

"Except your last trainee has not yet completed her certification," Silas said sharply.

John jerked around to glare at him.

"Silas, don't," Lucy said.

"There's no sense in denying it." Silas pulled a handkerchief from inside his suit coat and dabbed his face. "Besides, my division has the most extensive resources for—"

"So you keep saying," John snapped. "But I have yet to—"

"Stop. Just stop," I said loudly. "Yesterday, I didn't know about any of this or any of you. And now you want me to make some kind of decision? I don't even know what I'm choosing!"

"You need some time to think," Lucy said instantly.

"Not too much time." Silas tucked his handkerchief back into his pocket with a frown.

"This must be very overwhelming, I'm sure," John said. No kidding.

"You have our number," he continued. "We hope you'll be in touch with *one* of us soon." He gave Silas a glare.

I nodded. Yeah, yeah. Right away. After I'd had a chance to sort through everything they'd just dumped on me . . . and maybe taken a look through the boxes and papers my dad had left behind in the basement. I wanted some independent verification on all of this. I got the distinct sense that they might have told me just about anything to get me to come with them.

I walked out through the theater front doors, after Lucy demonstrated they weren't nearly as boarded shut as they had seemed at first glance, but I had to double-back to the rear of the building for my car.

Mina was leaning against her car when I slipped through the fence into the empty lot.

"Are they fighting over you yet?" she asked as I walked by.

I didn't say anything.

"Yeah." She smiled tightly, her face pale in the glare of the theater's security light. "Thought so. You are cash money, my friend."

I stopped. "What's that supposed to mean?"

She straightened up. "The better the talent in your region, the more jobs you can take, the more money you make."

"They didn't say anything about that."

"Of course not. It's all about the mission, right?" She rolled her eyes at my apparent stupidity. "All of them work other jobs. My dad's in construction. Lucy's a real estate agent in L.A. Silas does something with a bank. The more they make for the Order, the less they have to contribute out of pocket to the cause."

"There have to be others who—"

"We're a dying breed. Every generation the gift gets weaker. The Order is going to have to relax their standards soon, or there'll hardly be any full members after they're gone," she said, tipping her head toward the theater. "Except, of course, for you, the wunderkind, who actually ended up with real talent even with only one gifted parent. The *rest* of us . . ." She shrugged.

"You make it sound like you're half blind. You can still see and hear the . . . echoes." That term did not sound right. Just the taste of it my mouth felt . . . wrong.

"Yes, and if they hold perfectly still, I can catch them just fine," she said mockingly.

"Catching them is not everything. You can help in other ways."

"By being friends with them, like you?" She grinned at me. "Bet you didn't tell them that, did you, superstar?"

I looked away.

"You're going to have to choose, you know. The Order doesn't exactly endorse freethinking like that."

I edged closer to her, touched her chin to tip her face

to the light. The bruise looked worse in the stark shadows. "And this is how they show it?"

She pulled away. "Training exercises."

"Right," I said. "Your dad?" John had seemed like a nice enough guy, except when he'd yelled at Mina. Then . . . it had been like a glimpse of someone or something else under the surface. I had a hard time seeing my dad, who'd been the most laid-back parent I knew, being friends with him.

She glared at me. "No. I told you. Training. I didn't move fast enough." She let out a breath. "I'm never quite fast enough."

"You could leave," I said. "You're over eighteen, and—"

"And go where? Do what?" she demanded. "This is my whole life."

"It doesn't have to be."

"No." She shook her head. "All I need to do is pass this last test, and I become a full member. Then I can go anywhere," she said. "I can move to Lucy's territory or even Silas's." Mina rolled her eyes, but there was a wistful edge in her voice.

She seemed to hear herself then, and she straightened up, folding her arms across her chest.

"You worry about your own problems, Casper lover. Let me deal with mine." She gave me a ferocious smile. "After all, I'm not the one who has to explain all of this to her majesty."

That was a good point.

❧ 10 ❧

Alona

Even though it was the middle of the night, the hospital kicked things up into high gear for the miraculous recovery of coma girl. There were CAT scans, MRIs, X-rays, blood work, reflex tests, and a sleepy neurologist, with truly spectacular bed head, paged from home.

In some ways, it was almost worse than the last couple months of being invisible. Everyone asking me how I was doing, did this hurt, could I wiggle my toes, and telling me not to be afraid. All this intense attention and caring focused on a me that was not really *me* . . . and I couldn't escape it. It was almost torture. Here's what you want, but *you* can't have it.

Mrs. Turner stayed with me through all the tests and scans. She followed where she could and waited outside doors like the most persistent of guard dogs until the nurses or technicians brought me back within her sight. It was both reassuring (I didn't want someone to forget about me in a corner somewhere when I couldn't exactly speak up and remind them) and kind of sad.

It was like she was afraid Lily was going to disappear . . . or go back to sleep. She was right, of course, even if she didn't know it yet. I felt bad about that. She seemed like a nice enough woman, her horrible taste in sweaters aside. She didn't deserve to have her hopes crushed—as they inevitably would be once I got out and Lily went back to "sleep." And I *would* get out. I refused to contemplate any other possibility. It was just a matter of when and how.

During one of the breaks in testing, I'd used one of the many Ouija boards to painstakingly spell out a request for Mrs. Turner to call Will's cell—she'd had Lily's phone charged and waiting in the bedside table, just waiting for this day . . . or rather the day she thought it to be: the return of her daughter.

The call had gone to voice mail, but she'd left Will a message, telling him Lily was awake and asking for him.

That should have been more than enough to trigger a callback, or, more likely, a frantic visit to find out what was going on, because I knew he thought Lily was gone, far beyond the point of waking up and asking for anything.

But no, not yet.

"Are you doing okay?" Mrs. Turner asked, when we got back to my room—no, Lily's room—after the last test.

I nodded, a new skill I could add to my repertoire. Dr. Bedhead (I couldn't remember his real name) was "amazed" at Lily's sudden improvement, progress that could not be justified based on early test results. Medically, there were signs of increased and unusual brain activity—something I did not want to contemplate—but nothing that would allow Lily to be awake and moving around like this. Meanwhile, with every hour that passed, I gained more and more control over her body, which was freaking me out.

Hurry up, Will, hurry up. I repeated the words over and over in my head.

I was also starting to get a little bit grumpy. I was tired, my head hurt—or Lily's did, and I could feel it—and I'd just discovered, during one of the many times I'd been bodily shifted from a gurney to one machine or table or another, that while Lily Turner might have a waist even smaller than mine, her hips and thighs were enough to make me run screaming. If I, you know, could actually *run* anywhere.

Lily was all curves and soft where I'd had very hard-earned muscles. God, it was awful.

Look, I understood that she'd been in a coma for months and months. So, call me shallow, accuse me of being cruel to an injured girl, whatever. This wasn't my body. I didn't like it, didn't want it. Being trapped inside of it was like . . . well, wearing my worst fears on the outside. Not that anyone knew it was me in here, but *I* did.

"Lots of tests, but you should be done for a while now," Mrs. Turner continued, squeezing my hand reassuringly as she resumed her seat next to my bed.

Thank God. I was surprised we weren't glowing green from all the radiation, contrast, dye, and whatever else had been shot into us over the last few hours.

"Do you feel like trying to get some rest?" she asked warily, clearly caught between motherly instinct and her own fears of what might happen if I . . . we went to sleep. Honestly, I wasn't too sure either, nor did I want to find out. What if I got stuck, down in that darkness again, and couldn't find my way back up? This was not ideal, but it was better than that.

I shook my head in answer. It was getting easier and easier to do that.

"How about some television?" she suggested, reaching for the remote.

She turned on the television and flipped to a channel with an infomercial about a juicer.

I relaxed a little into my pillows. It was kind of nice being taken care of instead of always taking care of someone else. A novelty for me, really. Even though my experience with Lily's family had only been over the last few hours, I'd seen enough to make me the teensiest bit jealous. They cared about her. They didn't throw her things away even when it looked like she might not come back. Heck, they'd re-created her entire room here at the hospital. There'd been no garbage bags full of her belongings, no donations to the Salvation Army of her most precious memories. And she'd been in this irreversible coma a LOT longer than I'd been dead.

If it had been me in this coma instead of Lily . . .
You'd be here by yourself.

I shoved that thought away, even though I knew it was true. When I was fourteen, I fell from the cheerleading pyramid at practice—stupid Ashleigh Hicks and her wobbly knees—and hurt my wrist. Coach had taken me to the hospital for X-rays, but she couldn't stay. They'd tried to reach my parents, but no one had answered at my mom's house (shocker) and my dad was in Germany (or possibly the Days Inn downtown with his then mistress, now wife, and not taking any calls to keep up with the illusion of international unavailability).

I could have called friends or whomever I was dating at the time—I don't even remember who that was now—but who wants to put their family's dysfunction on display like that? *Hi, my parents are so messed up, they don't even care that I'm in the hospital?* I'd have sooner invited them over to my house to watch my mother stumbling around in her bathrobe.

So, I'd taken a cab home with my arm in a sling. My dad only found out about it when the hospital sent a bill, and then he was pissed. Apparently, I'd used the wrong insurance card.

That would never have happened to Lily.

Whatever. None of that mattered now. I just needed to focus on getting out of here.

Why wasn't Will calling back? What if it was because he was with *her*, Mina, Miss Frizztastic? Just the idea made me sick. But even if he was, no way would he ignore a call about Lily. He knew better than that. So what was the deal? If she'd gotten him in some kind of trouble that I was going to have deal with, I would kill her. Then we'd see how *she* felt about getting boxed, wouldn't we?

Mrs. Turner turned the channel to some early morning news program, and the brighter flickering of the screen hurt my eyes.

The first time I'd ever seen Lily, she was staring blankly ahead at the television, the twin reflections of screen dancing in her glassy eyes. Was that still how she looked even with me in here?

I shuddered.

Maybe . . . but maybe not. Tyler had noticed some kind of difference in Lily. I wondered what it had been that had tipped him off. I couldn't ask—not even with the time-intensive and laborious "spell it out through the Ouija board" method. (That was seriously getting old, and fast, by the way.) Mr. Turner had left to take Tyler, who'd been more than a little shaken up, home a while ago. I'd scared Tyler, apparently. I hadn't meant to. Then again, it had worked and the Turners were no longer talking about taking Lily home to die . . . so I was going to count that as a win. She had to stay alive long enough for Will to get me out of here, at the very least.

I tried to shift to alleviate the dull ache and pressure all up and down my left side, but I couldn't quite manage that much movement yet. Nor did I really want to be here long enough to attain that new level of skill. And yet, the cell phone on the bedside table next to me stubbornly refused to ring.

Mrs. Turner caught me staring at the phone.

"He hasn't called back, I promise," she said. "I just checked it."

When? I hadn't seen her do it.

"You're scowling at me," she said with wonder in her voice.

Yeah, well, she should get used to it. How hard would it be for her to check it again and show me? I mean, seriously.

My fingers twitched with the desire to snatch the phone away and see for myself.

"I know what you're thinking," she said, amused. "I'm still your mother."

Uh, nope.

"Go ahead. If you can get it, you can have it." She nudged the phone a few inches closer to me, but it was still much farther away than Tyler's wrist had been.

After one final glare at her, which seemed to have no effect on her serenity, I summoned all of my effort and made a lurching sideways grab for it.

The phone skittered away from my fingertips and plunged toward the floor. Mrs. Turner caught it before it hit.

She put it back on the nightstand and then shifted me by the shoulders in the bed until I was upright again. "Give it another try."

When she could just hand it to me? Why? What was this, some kind of game to her?

I frowned at her, which didn't seem to bother her at all.

"It's okay," she said. "You don't have to, if it's too hard."

Right. If I wanted that phone, I would get it. Period. I took a deep breath, focused on the phone, and tried to control my slide/fall toward it. This time I managed to lock my fingers on it before it slipped away.

I shrieked in frustration on the inside, but nothing louder than an annoyed huff escaped my lips.

Mrs. Turner just put the phone in place and set me to rights again without a word.

It occurred to me then that she *was* actually playing a game of sorts. She was using something I wanted to push me into further progress.

How wonderful for her and Lily. But just give ME the damn phone! I didn't want further progress. I wanted Will and I wanted out!

I locked gazes with Mrs. Turner, doing my best to convey that sentiment without words.

A knock on the door startled both of us. My head whipped around, the response time almost as fast as if it had really been me rather than me in a Lily shell.

A priest stood in the doorway, his hand still raised in the knocking position. "I'm sorry. I didn't mean to disturb you."

"Of course not, Father. My daughter and I were just having a disagreement." She smiled at me fondly, which made me want to kick her. I would not be so easily dismissed.

"I'm Father Hayes, the chaplain here at St. Catherine's. I was visiting another patient down the hall, and I heard about your daughter's miraculous recovery. I had to come and see for myself." He gave us a shaky and uncertain smile.

Um, okay, Father. You've had your glimpse of miracle me. Now, go away so we can get back to the matter at hand.

But oh, no . . . it couldn't be that easy.

"Come in." Mrs. Turner waved him forward. "I'm Corrine Turner. This is my daughter, Lily."

He stepped farther into the room and nodded at us. His gaze met mine for a bare second before it bounced away swiftly, focusing on Mrs. Turner.

"Is it true she was in a coma for almost a year?" he asked. His Adam's apple bobbed above his collar like it was an independent creature trying to escape his throat.

What was making him so jumpy? Also, hello, I am here and can hear you.

"Since last September," she said.

"Now she's awake. Just like that?" he asked, sounding more concerned than overjoyed.

Mrs. Turner didn't seem to notice. "Yes," she said, beaming.

"And they have no idea why. The tests—"

"Don't show anything yet, but as you know, some things are still beyond the understanding of science."

"God truly works in mysterious ways," he said with a tight smile.

I was not liking the vibe I was getting from him.

"Can I ask, have you noticed any . . . changes in her personality or unusual behavior?" he asked in a rush.

What the hell? I stared at him, and once more, his gaze darted toward me and then away just as quickly, like he was afraid to look at me for too long. Did he . . . actually suspect something was going on? I supposed in a technical sense what I'd done could be seen as a form of possession, even though that was far from what I'd intended. And priests and possession, well, I didn't need Will and his bottomless bank of movie trivia to know there was a history, to say the least.

Mrs. Turner cocked her head to one side with a laugh. "My daughter has been awake for only a few hours after coming out of what was called an irreversible coma. I'd say all of it has been unusual, wouldn't you?"

"Of course." He shook his head, flustered.

"Is there something in particular you're asking about, Father Hayes?" For the first time since the start of the conversation, Mrs. Turner's voice held a hint of suspicion.

"No, no." He raked a hand through his sandy brown hair before seeming to realize what he was doing and making a belated attempt to smooth it down. "Just trying to find pieces of hope in her story to share with other patients who might need it."

She nodded slowly, not convinced. "It's hard to know what her experience has been since she hasn't started talking yet. . . ."

And if I was talking, I'd be finding one of many ways to tell him to . . . "Go away." The words escaped my lips, shocking me more than anyone. I'd been thinking them hard enough to actually give them voice. Lily's voice, in fact, which was lower and huskier than my own.

"Lily!" Mrs. Turner sounded both thrilled and horrified.

"It's okay," he said with a laugh that sounded more like a nervous dog's bark than anything related to true humor.

"For someone who's been through as much as your daughter, I certainly understand wanting to be left alone. She deserves some peace, and it's up to the rest of us to make sure she gets it," he said, his stare boring through me like a warning.

Was he attempting to threaten me with an exorcism? Ha, bring it. Except . . . wait, what happened to exorcized spirits? If it was just getting me out of Lily, fine. But if it was intended to get rid of me by sending me into oblivion? No, thanks.

"Um, yes," Mrs. Turner said, now sounding flustered herself. "Speaking of which, it's probably best if she focuses on getting some rest now."

In other words, *leave*, dude.

He nodded, getting the message. Finally.

"A quick blessing, first?" he asked, but he was already standing over me before either of us could answer. His thumb, cool and kind of clammy, traced a cross on my forehead lightly while he murmured words of blessing.

He jerked his hand back as soon as he was finished, as though he expected me to go up in flames. And frankly, I wasn't sure that he was wrong. Except that I'd been in the light once and then I'd been sent back here, not wiped out of existence. So, I couldn't be so bad, right?

In any case, nothing happened, which seemed to confuse him. And it was probably a good thing I didn't have more control over Lily's body because I might have been tempted to throw myself around a bit on the bed, just to mess with him.

Mrs. Turner stood up. "Thank you so much, Father. We certainly appreciate your time."

He nodded again and slowly backed toward the door until he'd gotten some distance from me. Then and only then did he turn and leave the room, rather abruptly and without another word.

She sighed and sank back down into her chair. "Sometimes I just don't know where they find these people who work for the church."

I waited until I was pretty sure the priest was gone. "Call Will's house," I said, carefully enunciating, but even still, the *S*s dragged out too long.

Mrs. Turner tipped her head at me. "You're a regular chatterbox now, Lils."

"Call."

"Lily, it is four in the morning," she said with exasperation. "I'm not going to call their house and wake everyone up."

Except I happened to know that Julia worked the early morning shift at the diner most days and was likely already up anyway. "Please. Need Will."

She softened. "I'll call when it's reasonable, after eight at the earliest." She reached out and squeezed my hand with a reassuring smile. "But, honey, what you need to tell him, I'm sure he already knows."

I seriously doubted that.

❧ 11 ❧

Will

"**W**here is she?" A loud female voice demanded, and for a second, I thought Alona had somehow found out about Mina already and was preparing to do some damage to one or both of us.

But when I forced my sleep-gritty eyes open, it wasn't Alona, but Liesel standing in my bedroom just in front of my door. My *closed* door. You'd think she'd have taken that as a hint, but I'd long ago learned ghosts weren't much on subtlety.

I groaned. It was early—the sky outside my windows still a predawn gray—and two nights of little or no sleep was beginning to wear on me and my patience. "What do you want, Liesel?"

She folded her arms over her chest and stalked to the

foot of my bed, her dress rustling loudly. "She didn't even talk to you about us, did she?"

I struggled to focus and sit up. "Who?"

"Alona!"

Something about this was ringing a bell, dimly. Alona *had* mentioned something about Liesel yesterday morning, but nothing specific. I shook my head.

"I knew it," she spat. "She's always sabotaging me. I bet she didn't even tell you about Claire and Todd."

Todd? Who was Todd? No, I did not care. I wasn't awake enough yet to care. I rubbed my hands over my face. "Where's Eric?" I asked, realizing suddenly that he wasn't with her. No one has ever accused me of being my best in the morning.

She looked away with a sniff. "He couldn't be bothered. I don't know why; it's only our whole afterlife at stake."

Or maybe he knew something she didn't, which I suspected to be the case. Eric and I had had a couple of conversations over the last few weeks—usually while Liesel and Alona were sniping at each other—which had led me to believe that Mrs. Pederson and her love life (or lack thereof) might not be Liesel and Eric's biggest obstacle.

"You need to talk to Eric," I said wearily, "and you need to not be here when Alona shows up." Because I seriously did not want to witness the inevitable fallout when Alona discovered Liesel had come here without permission.

I glanced at my clock to see how much time was left, and stopped dead. It was 7:58 a.m.

I felt a surge of alarm and leaned closer to make sure I was reading it correctly. I was. Another check of the window revealed rain on the glass. What I'd taken for early morning was, in fact, just the start to an overcast day.

"What's wrong with you?" Liesel asked with great disdain.

"Did you see Alona?" I demanded. "Was she here?"

"This morning?" she asked.

I nodded, feeling like my head might bobble off in my anxiousness to answer and get her response.

"I just walked in a few minutes ago. Nobody was here but you," she said, staring at me as if I was crazy.

But I wasn't. Alona was late, fifty-five minutes to be exact, and that *never* happened. It couldn't. She showed up here every morning at precisely 7:03 a.m., the time of her death. It was a function of our ghost-talker/spirit guide bond.

Something was wrong. Fighting a feeling of panic, I stood up, snatched my jeans from the floor, pulled them on, and started tearing through the laundry on the floor, looking for my shoes. They seemed to have disappeared into one pile or another last night when I'd kicked them off.

"What is going on?" Liesel asked.

"Alona's missing," I said grimly. She'd left here yesterday all full of fire and some kind of plan for vengeance (against me, of course). Something must have happened. I envisioned her seeking out Mina to tell her exactly what she thought about Mina's hair, among other things.

Oh, God. That would probably get her boxed for sure. But Mina would have mentioned an event like that last night, wouldn't she have? Or maybe not—considering all that had happened. I could easily see Mina waiting to drop that little tidbit of information at exactly the time that would benefit her the most.

"How do you know she didn't just quit?" Liesel asked.

I stopped my frantic search for footwear and looked up at her. "What do you mean?"

She shrugged. "Alona shows up here every morning because she's your spirit guide, right?

"Yeah, so?"

"So, maybe she's not here because she quit." Liesel sounded a little too self-satisfied.

"And *why* would she do that?" I asked through gritted teeth.

"Because I told her one day you were going to toss her over for someone who was alive, that she was just convenient for now," Liesel said.

"Damn it, Liesel!" I couldn't believe this.

"What? That's not true?" She eyed me shrewdly. "You know it is. You aren't going to spend the rest of your life—"

"My life is none of your business," I snapped. "When did this happen?

"Two nights ago."

No wonder she'd reacted so badly yesterday morning, with Liesel filling her head with all this crap. Not that Alona ever would have been happy that I'd been out with Mina or that I was turning down her request about her parents, but she might not have been quite as apoplectic about it.

"This is your fault," I said to Liesel, pointing the one Chuck I'd managed to find, so far, at her.

"Me?" she asked, laying an offended hand on her chest. "What did I do?"

A knock sounded at the door. "Will, is everything okay in there?" my mom asked. "I heard shouting."

I grimaced. Of course; the one morning she didn't have the early shift at the diner. "I'm fine. I'll be right out," I called, and then stepped closer to Liesel. "You haven't seen Alona since?" I asked in a quieter voice.

"Would I be here looking for her if I had?" she asked in a rather snotty tone.

Fine. Whatever. I sat down to jam my shoe on, and by virtue of sheer luck, discovered my missing one by sitting on it. Excellent.

I needed to find Alona to make sure she was all right, at least. If, after that, she still didn't want to be my spirit guide . . . well, then, I'd have to deal with that when the time came. Just the idea, though, of her not being in my life was hard to imagine, and I didn't *want* to imagine it. I would miss her.

Ask me if I'd ever thought that would be possible a year ago. Hell, two months ago.

The trouble was, I had no idea where to begin searching for her. In theory, if she'd resigned as my spirit guide—could she even do that without me being aware of it?—then she'd probably woken up back on Henderson Street where she'd died. But that had been almost an hour ago. She could be anywhere by now.

My mom knocked again.

"Mom, I said I'm okay," I said, struggling to keep the irritation out of my voice.

"It's not that," she said, opening the door. She looked pale, standing there in a tattered plaid flannel robe with the house phone clutched to her chest. I hadn't even heard it ring.

"Is everything all right?" I asked, with the sudden sick assurance that it wasn't.

She nodded, her eyes bright with tears. "It's the hospital. St. Catherine's."

Oh. Oh, no. Lily. It felt like all the air had knocked out of me suddenly, even though I'd been expecting this call for months now. I nodded numbly. "When did she die? Last night or—"

"No, no, sweetie." My mother swept into the room and knelt to give me a one-armed hug. "It's not that. She's awake! Lily's awake."

I stared at her. "Lily Turner?"

My mother laughed. Her tears had clearly been of the happy variety. "Of course. How many other Lilys do you know?" She held the receiver out to me. "Her mother's on the phone. She says Lily has been asking for you."

But that was just not possible. I'd looked everywhere for her spirit after that accident. Lily was gone. Not dead, but certainly not alive and definitely not capable of waking up and asking for me.

And yet, I doubted that her mother, Mrs. Turner, would ever in a million years make something like that up.

So . . . what did that leave? I had no idea.

My head swimming, I stood up and took the phone.

"You." I pointed at Liesel. "Don't go anywhere." She'd helped cause this problem with Alona; she would help me solve it, by God.

My mom raised her eyebrows at me but said nothing.

Liesel flung herself, sulking, down at the foot of my bed, "Whatever. You better be ready to help Eric and me after this. This thing with Todd isn't going to last forever."

Todd again, whoever the hell he was. I ignored her and put the phone to my ear.

"Hello?"

"Will, it's Mrs. Turner. Lily would like to—"

In the background, I could hear a ruckus, a familiar voice, one I hadn't heard in almost a year and thought I'd never hear again, saying something in a demanding tone. It sent a chill over my skin. If I'd been wrong about Lily's spirit being gone, God, what else had I been wrong about? I'd been so sure. . . .

"In a minute, Lily," Mrs. Turner said, sounding slightly muffled.

"She's still a little hard to understand sometimes," Mrs. Turner said to me. "But we're working on it. She's been asking for you, pretty much since the moment she woke up. I made her wait until it was a decent hour, and as you can hear, she's not happy with me." And yet the joy in Mrs. Turner's voice, that her daughter was awake and annoyed with her, was evident.

"I'll put her on now," she said. The phone rattled a little, and I heard Mrs. Turner say, "Here you go, honey," in the distance.

"Will?"

Even though I'd been expecting it, hearing Lily say my name sucked the air out of my lungs and made my eyes sting with tears.

"Yeah," I managed.

"I need to see you." She was enunciating carefully, but other than that she sounded almost, well, normal. "Can you come to St. Catherine's, please? Now?"

I heard her mother admonishing her in the background for the demand. But Lily persisted. "Now?"

"I'm on my way," I said.

Lily Turner had moved to Groundsboro about a year and half ago from a small town in Indiana. With her conservative clothes and heavy, almost southern accent, she hadn't fit in at our school, which worked out well, since neither had I. Most people had assumed I was goth. In truth, I was just trying to be as invisible as possible. Dark clothes, earbuds in all the time, quiet in class—it was my way of disappearing. I'd been trying to avoid attracting the attention of all the ghosts wandering the halls, but it had worked equally well at repelling most of the living as well.

I liked Lily, though. She was different. I'd been going to school with the same people since kindergarten, and most of the time it was like they'd all been brainwashed by the same cult leader. Any sparks of real personality were snuffed out by the need for conformity within all the little individual cliques.

Jocks wore their letter jackets on certain days. The band kids created goofy T-shirts with sayings nobody else understood. Alona's crowd rose to the top by shoving everyone else down.

But Lily was an outsider. She asked smart questions and really listened to the answers, offering opinions that might not have been the "right" ones. She didn't know the right ones, not for our school. Not in the beginning, at least.

She was pretty, too, though not in the same fantasy crush way Alona was. She was more like the girl you'd want as your lab partner and your date for Homecoming, even if all you were going to do was sit at a table in the back and watch with amusement as the popular girls wept and raged over their loss in the race for queen.

At one point, I'd thought there might be something between us, a chance for it to be more than friends.

In the end, though, things had changed, the way they always do. Lily had harbored a secret obsession with the first-tier (a.k.a. popular people)—seeing them like Hollywood royalty. In the beginning, I think it was just because she'd never seen anything like them before, except in television and movies. Her high school had consisted of a hundred kids total, and they'd known one another since birth. So, pretty much all the mystery and intrigue was gone. But not here at Groundsboro High: here we had mystery, intrigue, and drama—oh, the never-ending drama—to spare. It was like watching a soap opera play out before your very eyes . . . or living in one.

Unbeknownst to me, our mutual friend Joonie, one of Lily's only other friends, had had a crush on Lily from day one. She took a chance one afternoon and confessed her feelings to Lily with a kiss. Though Lily tried to handle it the right way and let Joonie down kindly, Joonie's home life (nothing was ever good enough for her controlling and conservative minister father) was such shit that she kind of freaked, afraid her dad would find out what had happened.

Accusations and threats were made, and the two of them stopped speaking without ever telling me what had happened. Lily left us and started hanging about the edges of the popular crowd, seeking scraps of their begrudging acceptance. And then Ben Rogers, dickhead extraordinaire, had plucked her out of obscurity. He "dated" her for about a month, and then he dumped her publicly at a first-tier party.

Lily had been devastated, realizing finally that Ben and his crowd weren't as wonderful as everyone seemed to think. She'd left that party in tears and tried to call both Joonie and me on her way home. Then she'd missed a turn on her drive and slammed into a tree. She'd never woken up from that night.

Until today, apparently.

On the way to the hospital, I pushed the Dodge well over the speed limit, risking a ticket. I couldn't shake the irrational fear that somehow she would be unconscious again if I took too long to arrive.

Calm down. If she's awake now, she'll be awake in fifteen minutes.

Except maybe not. After Lily's accident, I'd done a ton of reading about comas and people coming out of them (or not). Sometimes the person woke up for a day or even just a few minutes, seemingly coherent, only to lapse back into that unnatural sleep . . . or worse yet, to die. I'd read of that happening—the person waking up only to die shortly afterward—at least a couple of times. The articles had interpreted the occurrence each time as a gift from God for that person to have a chance to say good-bye.

I hoped like hell that wasn't what was happening here. Though, honestly, I wasn't sure what to think about any of this. Until this morning, Lily waking up even to say good-bye and then die had been far from the realm of possibility in my mind.

It was a relief, finally, to see the hospital in the distance, and then to turn into the entrance. *Almost there.*

Of course, it seemed like everyone in the world must have been at the hospital on this particular Wednesday, because the parking garage was full, and the lots were jammed with cars.

After ten minutes of prowling for a space in the visitor section, I finally gave up and pulled into the vast empty expanse that was reserved for outpatient parking. Mine was the only car in the entire row. Far more visitors today than patients, I guess. Whatever. Let them tow me. It would be worth it just to get inside.

I got out of the car and jogged to the main entrance, keys jangling in my hand. I didn't even want to take the time to stuff them in my pocket.

The overwhelming stench of antiseptic and hospital filled my nose as soon as I pushed through the revolving door into the lobby. I hauled ass past the visitor information center in the middle of the lobby. I'd been here more than enough times to know where I was going, and though I probably technically should have registered as a visitor, I didn't have patience for that this morning.

In accordance with everything else, the elevator took forever to descend, and then once I was on it, another eternity to reach the fifth floor.

When the elevator doors started to open, I twisted sideways to fit through and hurried down the hall, my Chucks squeaking on the newly mopped floor.

I heard Lily before I saw her, her voice drifting out into the hall. "And *I'm* saying I don't care. I'd be more comfortable in my own clothes." She sounded kind of pissed.

Being in a coma had certainly made Lily more strident. If there'd ever been anything that bothered me about her, besides her obsession with that asshat Rogers and his crowd, it was that she tended to roll with things as they happened, assuming everyone else knew better than she did. Not anymore, apparently.

When I reached her open door, the sight inside was still a bit of a shock. Lily was sitting up in the bed without any visible means of support, though she was listing slightly to one side, and glaring daggers at a doctor whose hair stood up in all directions, like every strand was trying to escape his head at the same time. Mrs. Turner sat at her bedside, just like usual, only it seemed like she might float away with happiness. She seemed physically lighter, less beaten, now unburdened by the worry for her only daughter.

Lily looked . . . good. Different somehow, though. Maybe it was just the color in her cheeks and the furious glint in her eyes, or simply that it had been so long since I'd seen her in anything but a dull and insensate state. But it seemed more than that, like someone had lit a fire within her.

I knocked on the door frame and watched as heads turned in my direction.

Relief, as clear as I'd ever seen it, washed over Lily's face. "Thank God," she said, which was a little weird. If anything, shouldn't that be my line? I wondered what she was thinking for her to have that reaction. What did she remember about that last night? Did she think I'd avoided her call, still angry at her as Joonie had been?

"Hi," I said, feeling a bit awkward for the first time. It occurred to me right then that I hadn't so much as brushed my teeth before leaving the house. I'd showered last night after coming home from the theater, so at least I was relatively clean. But my arms were visibly scraped up after my fall through the stage, and if I had to guess, I'd bet that my hair wasn't in any better shape than the doctor's. All in all, a fairly disreputable picture.

Mrs. Turner, dark circles under her eyes and looking a little frazzled, performed introductions. "Dr. Highland, this is Will Killian, the friend Lily has been so anxiously awaiting."

I nodded at the doctor, who seemed less than pleased at the interruption.

"Can we have a minute alone, please?" Lily asked.

"Don't be rude," Mrs. Turner scolded mildly. Then she turned her attention to me with a knowing smile. "I'm sure you have lots of catching up to do."

Lily rolled her eyes.

Mrs. Turner stood and made her way to the door, followed by Dr. Highland. "Don't be surprised if she doesn't remember some things," he said to me quietly as he passed. "She's having a little trouble with details."

"Just because I didn't remember a few names," Lily muttered.

"Including your own middle name?" Mrs. Turner inquired from the doorway.

Lily huffed.

"She's also experiencing some personality shifts," Dr. Highland said carefully. "Again, not uncommon in these types of head injuries."

I nodded.

"I'll give you a personality shift," Lily said under her breath.

Whoa. Okay . . .

"Just try not to upset her," the doctor said with one last exasperated look at Lily.

Then he and Mrs. Turner left, closing the door partially behind them.

Lily waved me closer, and I obeyed, moving to the side of her bed. "Listen," she said in an urgent whisper. "I know you're not going to like this, but I don't have time to break you into this gently. I need you to get me out of here."

"The hospital?" Who was this girl? The Lily I knew would never have dreamed of going against her mother and probably an entire team of doctors. "I don't know if—"

"No, not the hospital," she hissed impatiently. "Out of here." She gestured to herself, hands on her chest.

I shook my head, confused. "I don't understand."

She grimaced. "I was afraid of this."

She took my hand in hers and tugged me down to her until we were eye to eye.

"I'm not Lily, as you should damn well know," she said evenly. "Lily's gone. You're the one that told me that, remember?"

Cold washed over me, and the world spun. Pieces of two separate puzzles I'd thought unrelated snapped together, forming a complete picture. Alona missing. Lily unexpectedly and unbelievably awake and in possession of a personality that seemed nothing like what I'd known of her.

With my heart pounding too hard, I stared at Lily's familiar heart-shaped face—the sprinkle of freckles across her nose, the crinkles near the corner of her eyes that suggested her eagerness to laugh, the jagged but healing scar from her accident—and the equally familiar but definitely un-Lily-like determined glint in her light brown eyes, which were even now narrowing in that haughty yet almost sexy way that was the trademark look of disdain for only one girl I knew. . . .

"Alona?" I asked through numb lips.

❧ 12 ❧

Alona

I knew it would be bad when Will figured it out. That's why I'd kept my call for help so general. I couldn't take the chance he'd be so angry he wouldn't come to the hospital.

And yet somehow, seeing him make the realization, put all the pieces together, it was worse than I'd imagined. Maybe telling him on the phone would have been better.

He went pale, except for two spots of red high up on his cheekbones, and he looked like I'd punched him. No, he looked like I'd punched his mother and then stomped on him for good measure.

Will pulled back from me and dropped my hand like it was on fire.

I'd been expecting this, and yet it still hurt to see that

expression of disgust on his face.

"You did this to get back at me?" He wouldn't meet my gaze, and his fists were clenched at his sides.

His accusation shocked me. "No!" Okay, I'd set out to prove a point, but it wasn't that one. I'd just wanted to show him I didn't need him. Yet I'd accomplished the exact opposite.

He shot me a look brimming with fury and skepticism.

"Seriously, do you really think if I set this up to gloat, I'd be in a hospital gown?" I plucked at the loose pale blue fabric at my neck. "Things just got out of control."

"I can see that," he said tightly.

"Hey, this is your fault, too," I snapped.

"This ought to be good," he muttered, which kind of ticked me off. He really didn't see his role in all of this?

"If you hadn't gotten all caught up in G.I. Jane's propaganda about the living being more important than the dead, and just delivered my message like I'd asked, I wouldn't have been forced to go to these extreme measures," I argued.

"So, I tell you no and that's, what, a green light for you to start body-snatching my friends?" He scrubbed his hands over his face, and I noticed deep and angry-looking scrapes and cuts on the inside of his wrists and forearms. A twinge of concern made my chest tighten. When had that happened? Now was probably not the time to ask.

"First of all, it's *one* friend, and it's called body-*borrowing*." I sniffed. "I was only using her hand. You know, like when I SAVED YOUR LIFE?"

He rolled his eyes.

"Except . . ." I bit my lip. "Something different happened this time." I folded my arms across my chest, a gesture that felt both familiar and wrong at the same time. In keeping with her other curves, Lily's chest was noticeably bigger than mine. No wonder Will had liked her. Yeah, okay, he was a leg guy—trust me, it was obvious—but boobs were still boobs.

"Clearly something very different," Will said.

"Shut up," I snapped. "You weren't there. You don't know what it was like." I paused, shuddering at the memory of that complete and utter darkness I'd woken to. "Once it started pulling me in, I couldn't stop it. It didn't want to let go of me."

"You ever notice how this is everybody's fault but yours?" he asked.

I scowled at him. "Whatever. Just call me out of here, and then you can yell at me as much as you want, okay?" Well, not really, but whatever would get him to stop bitching and start summoning was a lie I could live with.

He hesitated and then shook his head slowly. "I don't think that's going to work."

I felt the first pulse of true panic. "Why not?"

"Because if you were still my spirit guide, you would have shown up this morning in my room, like usual," he pointed out. "Whatever you did . . . it changed things."

I shook my head. "You don't know that." I refused to accept that idea or the growing fear in my gut that he might be right. "Besides," I argued, "I didn't *do* anything. It just happened."

"You didn't stick your hand in hers?"

"Okay, fine, yes," I said with exasperation. "I did that, but I certainly didn't set out to take her entire body."

"No, that was just lucky," he said.

"Do you think I want to be in here?" I shouted. "This is the *last* body I would have picked for myself. It's short and fat and weak and—"

"I know at least one person who was pretty happy with it and might have enjoyed the opportunity to have it again," he said quietly.

I remembered belatedly that this was his friend. *Good, Alona. Piss him off further. That'll help.* "Look, I didn't mean ..." I gritted my teeth. "Can we please just stop arguing long enough to try to get me out of here?"

This *had* to work. It was my one and only plan. I didn't have other ideas, which was not like me, but this wasn't exactly a standard situation in which one could develop a backup plan or two, like what to do if you accidentally sit in spaghetti sauce in the caf.

Will's mouth tightened, but he moved around the bed and sat down in the visitor's chair that Mrs. Turner normally occupied. He took a deep breath and closed his eyes.

I waited a beat or two, but he didn't say anything. "Are you trying?" I asked.

"I'm trying to concentrate, yeah," he said, sounding annoyed.

I shut up.

A minute ticked by, and then another. I concentrated,

willing the sensation of being pulled free to wash over me. I wasn't quite sure what that would feel like, so I envisioned the resistance inside Lily's body, the force that had drawn me in, clinging to me like black mud even as Will yanked me out with a loud suction-releasing pop.

But the trouble was, I didn't actually *feel* anything, not pulled or tugged in any way. Not even a vaguely mystical tingle. Just the same tired, achy feeling that had been there since I'd woken up in charge of this body. *Crap.*

Will opened his eyes and met my gaze, though I thought he might have flinched a little in doing so. "It's not working," he said.

"Yeah, I noticed. Maybe you're not trying hard enough." I could hear the shrill edge of panic in my voice. "Can you try, like, reaching in and pulling me out?"

In answer, he reached over and looped his hand around my wrist, his touch warm and comfortingly familiar even though he was angry. "I'm not the one who could reach through people, places, and things, remember?" He waggled my captured arm at me.

"I can't stay in here," I whispered.

"You were certainly eager enough to get in," he said.

Tears filled my eyes and slipped down my cheeks with virtually no resistance. Crap, Lily was a crier. "You were leaving me behind, just like everyone else!" *Damn it, Alona, keep it together.* "What was I supposed to do?"

He raked his hands through his hair. "I don't know, but hijacking someone wouldn't have been on the top of my list."

"It wasn't on mine, either!" I wiped my face, the back of my hand jolting and bumping over the unfamiliar terrain.

He let out a slow breath. "And I wasn't leaving you behind. I hadn't made any decisions about—"

"The fact there's suddenly a decision that needs to be made kind of says it all, don't you think?" I asked.

"That doesn't justify—"

"I never said it did," I said quietly.

His expression softened a little bit, but that was it. He didn't hug me, didn't make a move to comfort me. Not that I expected that exactly. I'd known he wouldn't be in the forgiving mood anytime soon, if ever, but it didn't stop me from wishing that he would be. I could have used just a little sympathy, even if I didn't entirely deserve it. It wasn't like this was easy for me, either. But he was cold and distant, maybe even more than he'd been the first time we'd ever talked.

"We just need to figure this out," he said, rubbing his forehead like it hurt. "If you got in, there has to be a way to get you out."

"What about your books?" I asked.

He looked at me blankly.

"You have all those books at home about ghosts and the afterlife and—"

"Yeah, I'm pretty sure I didn't miss all the chapters on body-borrowing. And before you ask, I doubt there's an instructional video on YouTube." He shook his head. "I didn't even know this was possible." He frowned at me. "It must be something different about you. Or Lily, maybe. Or some combination. If ghosts could take bodies all the time, people would be nothing but a revolving door of spirits. We need more information on how this works."

I bit my lip, and then stopped, feeling horribly self-aware. That was not my nervous habit. When had I started doing that? My go-to fidget was to bite my thumbnail, though I'd spent years breaking myself of the habit.

"There was a priest here earlier," I offered finally. "He seemed to know something wasn't right. Like maybe he thought I was . . . well, Lily . . . was possessed."

He jerked back, as if considering this idea for the first time. "Possession."

I knew what he meant. This wasn't like any depiction of possession I'd ever seen, though Will had probably watched more of those movies than I had. But there was no struggle here, no violence, no head revolving backward. It was more like two seat-belt-buckle halves clicking together, just not necessarily the ones intended for each other.

"If I told Mrs. Turner to bring him back . . ."

"No," Will said immediately, and if possible, he turned a shade paler. I guessed that answered my question about what happened to exorcized spirits. Oblivion. Nothingness.

"Are you sure?" I asked. "Maybe if we asked him just to kind of, I don't know, do it halfway or not full power?" Maybe a mixture of holy water and tap water or something instead of the fully leaded version?

He stared at me. "Are you really so shallow that you'd risk being turned into nothing?"

"Are you really that determined to have your friend back?" I shot back.

He gave me a disgusted look. "Don't make it about that. You couldn't care less about her."

Mrs. Turner poked her head in the door, startling both of us. "Is everything okay?"

"Just another minute . . . Mom," I said, almost choking on the word.

She nodded and backed away, but I suspected she wasn't going far. "They're going to want to take her . . . me home soon," I hissed at Will. "I can't do that." Pretending to be someone else was exhausting, and for some horrible reason, I felt compelled to get it right. Or as close as I could. I hated seeing the occasional flashes of hurt and confusion that crossed Mrs. Turner's face when I behaved more like me and less like the daughter she knew. It made me feel like I was taking a test and failing with every question. I wasn't used to *failing* at anything. The idea of sitting at their kitchen table or whatever, trying to act like I recognized things and remembered people . . . God, I couldn't even imagine that kind of pressure.

"When?" Will asked.

"Tomorrow, maybe the day after." God, what if I was still stuck here then? Three days as Lily Turner? The last twenty-four hours had been more than enough.

"We've got a little time, then," he said, seemingly more to himself than to me.

"Time for what?" I asked.

But he just shook his head.

"You have an idea," I accused.

"Not a good one," he said grimly.

I sat up straighter, automatically correcting for my left side, which was weaker, thanks to the initial accident damage and the surgeries that had apparently followed. Lily had some serious scars, even beyond the one on her face. "I don't care. I'll do anything. Tell me."

But he just shook his head.

"What, so now you're keeping secrets?" I asked.

He glared at me.

Okay, so maybe not the best response in terms of avoiding hypocrisy, but this was my life at stake . . . sort of.

I had sudden flash of insight. "It doesn't involve *her*, does it?"

"Who?"

"Mina, Little Miss Rambo of the spirit world." I flung my hands out to encompass the room and everything beyond it.

He made a face. "It's a little more complicated than that."

"Which means, what, yes, you're going to tell her?" Panicked, I didn't even wait for his answer. "She'll box me for sure." Not existing would be bad. Existing as little separate pieces, each perhaps aware and alert forever, might be worse. "She got rid of Mrs. Ruiz just for slamming a few doors, so—"

"And almost killing me," he pointed out, turning to face me.

"—what do you think she's going to do to me when she

finds out about this?" I gestured down at myself.

"Maybe you should have thought about that before," he said.

I stared at him.

He grimaced, started to speak, stopped, then tried again. "She was my friend, Alona, and you didn't care. You did what you wanted, no matter who it hurt." He shook his head. "I thought you were changing, that you were different now, but I'm not sure anymore."

I felt tears sting my eyes again. "What are you saying?"

"I don't know." He lifted his shoulders helplessly. "I'm going to do my best to get you out of there because Lily deserves that, her family, too, even though it's probably going to kill her mom. But after that . . . I think maybe we should go our separate ways."

Even though I'd known this was a possibility, somehow it still took me by surprise and I couldn't breathe for a second. Tears poured, hot and wet, down my face, splashing down on the front of my hospital gown.

Will was unmoved. He stood up.

"I'll be back as soon as I can. Keep her phone with you."

He was leaving already? "What am I supposed to do while you're figuring out your big plan?" I tried to keep calm. It had not escaped my notice that he hadn't answered my question about Mina.

"Just keep doing what you've been doing."

I nodded, wiping my face on the edge of the sheet.

He started for the door, and then he stopped. "Was it

worth it?" he asked without turning around.

"What?"

"Doing this so you could talk to your parents? Force them back into mourning you?"

I flinched. He made it sound so cruel. I couldn't tell him the truth. I hadn't had many opportunities to even make the call with any kind of privacy, and the few I'd had . . . I hadn't been able to convince myself to take them. It was one thing to send Will with a message and watch the fallout at a bit of a distance. But now that I had the fingers to dial the phone and the capacity to speak to them and be heard directly . . . I was kind of afraid to hear what they would say. Will was worried that hearing from me would send them into a tailspin of grief. I was worried it wouldn't.

"Yes," I lied. What else could I say?

"I hope so," Will said. Then he left.

After a few seconds, Mrs. Turner stuck her head back in the door cautiously. "Okay if I come in again?"

I nodded, not quite trusting myself to speak.

She came farther in the room, moving toward her chair, but then she stopped, her head cocked to one side as she took in my expression and probably my tear-reddened eyes. I mean, what were the odds that Lily was attractive while crying when even *I* hadn't been able to manage that?

Her shoulders sagged, and she looked at me with such sympathy. "Oh, honey. It's just going to take some time."

I knew that she didn't even have a clue what was going on, but it didn't matter. Hearing the genuine caring in her voice made my eyes burn with tears again, and then I started to cry. Sob, actually. Big gulping, loud embarrassing sobs. Ones I'd never allowed myself in front of other people when I was alive.

Get it together, Alona. But I couldn't seem to make myself stop. It was like a faucet somewhere had snapped off, and everything was pouring out.

She moved to sit on the edge of my bed, pulling my head to rest on her shoulder. "It's okay. It's going to be fine." She repeated the words over and over again, which should have worked, except I knew that if I got what I wanted, it wouldn't be okay, it wouldn't be fine, at least not for her.

She stroked my hair. "You were friends with Will and then you weren't. And then the accident . . ." She rested her chin lightly on top of my head. "It's bound to be confusing for him. For both of you."

There was a knock at the door. I looked over to see Mr. Turner standing in the doorway awkwardly, a bouquet of wildflowers in one hand and the hugest bundle of brightly colored balloons in the other. He was wearing another denim shirt, in a lighter shade of blue this time. Tyler hovered at his side, looking a little less freaked than yesterday, but still wary. He was twisting a piece of white fabric in his hands.

"Is now a bad time?" Mr. Turner asked.

I felt Mrs. Turner stiffen next to me. "What are you doing here, Jason? What about—"

"I took the day off of work," he said quickly. "This deserves celebration."

"Oh," Mrs. Turner said in a small but happy voice.

He stepped closer, dragging the balloons across the ceiling.

"I didn't know if you still liked this kind of flowers or not," he said to me gruffly. "When you were little, you used to beg me to stop the car on trips to Grandma's house in Wisconsin so you could pick the flowers on the side of the road. I think those were mostly weeds, but these reminded me of them."

He thrust the flowers at me, and I took them. They were just cheap grocery store flowers still in the plastic, but they were pretty, and he'd picked them out himself. Whenever *my* dad had sent me flowers, they'd been huge, ornate arrangements and come from the most expensive florist in town . . . with a note in his assistant's handwriting. I'd thanked my dad once, and he'd had no idea what I was talking about. I was just an item on someone's to-do list.

Mrs. Turner gave a choked laugh. "They're beautiful, Jason. Really." She sounded like she was crying now, too.

"And Tyler has something for you, too." He waved his son over, who was still standing on the edge of the hall.

Tyler approached slowly. "You know that place in your room I'm not supposed to know about, where you hide the stuff I'm not supposed to touch?"

So this is what it was like to have a sibling. I nodded and hoped he wouldn't ask for details about said secret location or its contents.

"Here." He tossed the fabric he'd been twisting in his

hands at me. It fluttered down to land on top of my covers.

I picked it up. It was a piece of soft white satin, worn and tattered around the edges, and kind of grungy looking, but I knew that it was supposed to be important just by the way Tyler and Mr. Turner were watching me for my reaction. I picked it up carefully because it felt like it might fall apart. Whatever it was, it was either really old or really worn out, or both.

"You found Blankie," Mrs. Turner exclaimed.

Oh, this sounded embarrassing. But also important.

Without thinking, I looked to her for explanation and another of those sad expressions crossed her face. I'd failed another question on the Lily exam.

"Oh, right, Blankie," I repeated, feeling the heat rise in my cheeks. Clearly, there was some childhood memory associated with this thing. Logic would suggest it was, or had once been, an actual blanket, something Lily had evidently cherished enough to hide away from her brother. I liked the idea of having something with that kind of history. With my mother's manic and occasionally alcohol-fueled redecorating sprees, I'd rarely had any bedding in my room last long enough for the newness to wear off, let alone for a sentimental attachment to form.

I ran my fingers along the torn edge gently.

"A lot of children keep a scrap from their security blankets," Mrs. Turner said, her tone chiding yet approving. "You took it everywhere until about third grade, and even then you slept with it under your pillow, remember?"

I nodded. I could imagine it.

"I looked and looked for this when I was gathering up things to bring here to your room." She rested her head against mine for a moment. "I thought maybe it had gotten lost or you'd thrown it away. I was so upset."

Imagine that. A mom who wanted to keep things that had been important to her daughter.

Mrs. Turner folded the strip of fabric into my palm and closed my fingers over it, and then she kissed my forehead with a sigh that seemed to indicate now that Blankie and Lily had been reunited, all would be right with the world.

I looked away, staring at the far corner of the room so I wouldn't start crying again when I'd barely stopped. It wasn't fair. Why did Lily Turner get these parents, this family, and not me? She wasn't even around to appreciate them. She probably hadn't appreciated them even when she was around. Not as much as I would have.

❧ 13 ❧

Will

Alona Dare had stolen a body, and not just any body, though that would have been bad enough. No, she had to pick *Lily*.

It really shouldn't have surprised me. She always thought she was entitled to take whatever she wanted, and damn the consequences. But my God, of all the selfish things to do.

She'd said it was an accident and maybe it had been, but that didn't change the fact that she hadn't considered anybody else in this mess except for herself. That was vintage Alona Dare, right there.

I stalked back through the hospital and out to my car, fury fueling my stride. I was half-tempted to call Mina, let her show up in the room with all of her clanking boxes, and maybe Alona would freaking learn something.

But that wasn't my job. I wasn't the one responsible for teaching her. The light had sent her back; the light would decide if that had been a mistake, not me.

However, that didn't change the fact that I needed help.

I got to my car—it hadn't been towed, thank God—and climbed inside. I needed privacy and a second to think before taking any kind of next step.

I was willing to bet someone within the Order knew more about what Alona had done, not specifically that she'd done it but how it had happened and maybe how to undo it. The trouble was what they'd do with Alona afterward. No matter what I'd let Alona think, I would not be calling Mina in on this. No way. Removing and boxing Alona would be too much of a trophy for her to resist.

But the Order was still my best option for information. The only trick was how to get it without them descending upon the hospital and Alona and Lily. Mina had claimed Mrs. Ruiz was a green-level ghost, whatever that meant, but it insinuated that there were levels higher than that. And if I had to guess, I would say they'd classify Alona as belonging to one of those more powerful categories. Which meant the Order wasn't going to just let her walk away.

But that didn't mean I couldn't attempt a little subterfuge and see what I could learn. If I was careful, it would look like I was simply an eager student.

I reached into my pocket for the crumpled card with the 800 number on it.

Lucy seemed to be the most sympathetic among the Leadership and the most willing to overlook my dad's peculiar concern with the dead instead of—or in addition to—the living. She might be more willing to give me answers the others would dismiss as information I didn't need to know.

I pulled my mom's cell phone from my pocket. She'd insisted that I take it so I could call her and give her an update after my visit with Lily, which I'd have to do immediately after calling the Order. Otherwise she might freak out and start trying to track me down.

I flipped the phone open and started dialing the number for the Order, trying to organize my thoughts into a coherent story that didn't sound too suspicious.

It rang once and then a woman's efficient but nasal voice said, "Answering service."

I hadn't been expecting that. Not that I thought the Order would be trumpeting their name and purpose, but this generic greeting made me wonder for a second if I'd misdialed. "Um, hey, can you connect me with Lucy?" I realized belatedly that I didn't know Lucy's last name.

But this didn't seem to faze the operator. "One moment, please."

The connection clicked in my ear and then it started ringing again, tinny and distant. Hopefully, the woman was transferring me to Lucy's cell phone and not a desk phone out in California somewhere. I assumed that Lucy was still in town after last night, or maybe on her way back.

"Lucy Shepherd," she answered, sounding more professional and crisp than she had at the theater.

"Hi Lucy, it's Will . . . Killian," I added quickly.

"Will!" she cried with delight, so much so that the phone vibrated against my ear with the reverberations of her voice. I winced.

"I'm not interrupting anything, am I?" I asked. If she was in a meeting with John and Silas, I wanted to know. That might affect the answers she'd be willing to give me.

"Of course not, hon. I'm just packing up for my flight back this afternoon. What can I do for you?"

"I just had a couple of questions, if you don't mind."

"Oh, sure." Her voice softened. "I understand."

And I realized she thought I wanted to ask about my dad. I did—badly—but now was not the time. Except I couldn't help but think, what if there wasn't another time? Who was this Danny Killian that Lucy and the others knew? Like, as a person, not just the secretive and unhappy guy who was my dad?

"Will, are you still there?"

"Oh, yeah, sorry, just got distracted for a second." I needed to keep my focus on the immediate problem. Getting Alona free. "Listen, I know this is going to sound strange, but I'm just trying to wrap my head around everything, and I've been hearing some things I wanted to run by you."

"Okay," she said cautiously.

"Is it possible for a ghost to possess a person? Not what they show in movies, where everything is all crazy and split pea soup, but like almost undetectable? The person might seem normal or close to it."

She was quiet for a long moment, a silence that dragged out way too long. Shit, had I just given myself away? "Lucy?"

"You've been talking to Mina," she said with a sigh.

"What?" I asked, confused. "I mean, yeah, but not . . ."

"She's insisting that we take this priest's call seriously, but what she's forgetting is that red-level manifestations are very rare. I've never even seen one before and—"

"Wait, what priest?"

"The chaplain at St. Catherine's." Now she sounded confused. "Didn't Mina tell you that?"

Despite the heat in the car, I felt a sudden chill. Alona had mentioned a priest.

"Apparently, a girl who was in a coma for months and months woke up early this morning, and she's already talking and moving around."

Oh, no. No, no, no.

"That can be one of the signs," Lucy continued, oblivious to my distress. "Red-level echoes like that tend to go after weakened targets and make them their own. Like I said, though, they're incredibly rare."

"What is the Order doing about it?" I forced myself to ask in what I hoped was a normal voice or the closest thing to it that I could manage at this point.

"Do?" She laughed. "There's nothing to do. This is just that poor girl's attempt to win one more chance at full membership with a containment. But I doubt they'll find anything."

I froze. "They're looking to find something?" Looking was bad. Looking meant members of the Order with disruptors and boxes would be in the vicinity of Alona.

"I thought you said you'd talked to Mina," she said with a frown in her voice. "John took her to the hospital to check it out, even though—"

I snapped the phone shut, dropped it to the floor, and bolted from the car.

✤ 14 ✤

Alona

The strange thing about a hospital is that you'd think it would run on routine, the same thing every day, every hour.

Instead, it was more like they set out to throw random elements in at odd intervals just to keep you off balance.

Mr. Turner had just left to take Tyler to the cafeteria when an orderly showed up in my room with a wheelchair. "Physical therapy," he called out far too cheerfully as he pushed the chair up to my bed. His scrubs had dancing teddy bears on them. Blecch.

"Are you serious?" I asked. The last thing I wanted to do in this body was anything physical.

"Dr. Highland never said anything," Mrs. Turner spoke up with a frown.

The orderly was undeterred. "The sooner we start, the faster she'll be back on her feet."

"Okay," Mrs. Turner said, still uncertain. She set her book down, a tattered paperback that she carried with her everywhere without ever seeming to make progress in it, and stood up.

"It might be better for you to wait here. Therapy is hard on the patient, but sometimes it's even harder to watch," the orderly said.

Great. This sounded like more fun every minute.

"No, I think I should—" she began.

"I'll be okay," I said. Now that I could talk, I wasn't completely helpless. And it would probably be a good idea to start putting some distance between us. If Will could figure a way out of this—and he seemed determined, if more for Lily's sake than mine—then the less time we spent together now, the better. Not that it would help all that much after everything that had happened, but it wouldn't make things worse as further bonding might.

"Are you sure, baby?" Mrs. Turner asked with a frown.

The weird thing was the prospect of leaving Mrs. Turner here and going to therapy alone didn't exactly spawn the feelings of relief I'd expected. It was almost like I wanted her to go with me.

No, no, no. Not your body, not your life.

Not your family.

"Yes, I'm sure," I said firmly, trying to convince myself as much as her.

"Okay," she said, beaming.

Oh. She saw it as a sign of improvement. Fabulous. Well, at least it made her happy.

After some very awkward maneuvering that revealed far more of this body than I would have wanted if it were mine, the orderly managed to get me into the wheelchair. That alone was enough to exhaust me, even though I'd done little more than just keep my balance during the transfer.

He spun the chair around expertly to face the door, and only then did I realize I'd left Lily's cell phone on the bedside table. *Crap.* Well, how long could one physical therapy session last anyway? I'd probably be back before Will called.

If he called.

"Bye, Lilybean," Mrs. Turner called after us.

This girl had more ridiculous nicknames than I had cute shoes. Or, used to have. Whatever. I wondered if my mom had finished cleaning out my room. Were all my clothes and shoes already on the shelves at the Salvation Army, next to ugly plaid sports jackets and sensible heels that *nobody* wanted to wear?

I shoved that thought away. I had enough to worry about right now.

The orderly moved us down the hall swiftly, like we were running late or something. The momentum, especially around corners, made staying upright a little tricky. More than once I thought I'd slide right out of the chair into a big hospital-gowned heap on the footrests.

But I didn't ask him to slow down. Because every second

we cut off this little adventure was one less in the hallway where everyone stared at me as we passed by. Some of them even followed me down the corridor, whispering to each other.

Look, I get it. It looks like a miracle, talks like a miracle, but . . . it's not.

Reaching the service elevator—they never used the visitor elevators to move patients around, as I'd discovered during my bajillion tests earlier this morning—was, quite frankly, a relief.

Humming a tuneless collection of notes under his breath, the orderly wheeled me inside and pressed the button for the basement.

The basement? That seemed vaguely odd. Not that I had any clue where physical therapy took place, but I'd seen most of the basement at various times. After all, the morgue was down there, as was the MRI machine—another discovery from this morning.

Looking back on it, I should have asked. I should have spoken up and said something, anything. Maybe that would have been enough to push events back on course.

But I didn't. I was tired from the effort of sitting up during the (relatively) wild wheelchair ride, and honestly, at the hospital, with so many people pushing and pulling at you, taking you one place, only to drag you somewhere else, you kind of just surrender your destiny to the powers that be with the idea that they know what's best. I wasn't proud of it, but that was just the way it worked.

The orderly wheeled me out of the elevator and down the main corridor before turning off into a small hall I'd never noticed before.

He stopped in front of an unmarked door and knocked.

The door opened, and the first thing I noticed was the smell: mildew and fake pine. The orderly pushed me inside, and then I saw the mops standing in the metal bucket, the rusting and tilted shelf that held crusty-looking bottles of industrial cleaners, and a huge washtub.

Father Hayes stood next to the industrial tub, his hands folded at his waist, as though he'd been praying while waiting for us.

"What's going on?" I demanded, feeling the first spark of fear. Though somehow, in the back of my head, I was still thinking that this must be a mistake. A wrong turn.

"Raymond, thank you." He stepped forward and extended his hand toward the orderly who shook it. "You are truly doing the work of the Lord."

Oh, this was not good.

I craned my neck around to find Raymond or as much of him as I could see from that awkward angle. He released the priest's hand and turned to leave. He was just going to abandon me down here in the janitor's closet! "No, no, no. Come back, Raymond. Take me out of here. What about physical therapy?"

But he just kept going, at a speed much closer to normal rather than the rapid rate at which he'd moved before. And that's when I realized he hadn't been doing that to spare me embarrassment or discomfort. Nope, he'd been trying not to get caught. *Bastard.*

The door snapped shut behind Raymond, and I twisted around to face Father Hayes again, but he wasn't looking at me. His attention was focused on something behind me.

"I assume this space will be adequate for your needs?" he asked.

I turned the other way, straining my neck to see who he was talking to, and as soon as I did, my breath caught in my throat and my heart exploded into a frantic beat. There, where the door would have hidden her from sight, stood Mina, scourge of the spirit world. She had her huge duffel bag strapped over her shoulder, and her curly hair stood out around her head in a frizzy halo. And, in her right hand, she held the shiny disruptor weapon that had taken down Mrs. Ruiz, aimed right at me.

Will. Had he called her down on me?

I wanted to throw up, not just from the fear but the betrayal. He'd threatened it, but I never actually thought he'd go through with it.

Mina moved to block the door. "This is fine," she said to Father Hayes, her weapon hand steady and unwavering. She reached up and removed her duffel with her free hand, setting it down on the ground with a loud clanking sound.

But if Will was responsible, where was he? He might leave me to Mina, but he would never abandon Lily to chance. And what was the priest doing here? This made no sense.

"I think there's been some kind of mistake," I said, trying

to sound levelheaded, the way a regular person would if she found herself in a janitor's closet with seemingly crazy people instead of physical therapy.

"No. No mistake," Mina said, circling me. "I can almost see you in there, flickering just under the surface." She leaned over, bringing the disruptor closer to my face. I didn't know if it would work on me in this form, but I was pretty sure it would, or else she wouldn't be pointing it at me.

"Touch me with that, you freaky-haired bitch, and I will make you regret the day you decided to home perm," I snapped.

Mina stopped, her mouth hanging open. Then she cocked her head to the side, an evaluating look on her face. "Highness? Is that you in there?"

Damn.

"*You're* the red level." She grinned. "This is going to be fun." She backed up from me and knelt down by her duffel, careful to keep her attention on me. With her free hand, she started pulling out little metal boxes, ones I recognized as similar, if not identical, to the ones from the front room of the Gibley Mansion.

This was it. Mina was going to haul me out, box me up in little pieces, and stick me on a shelf somewhere.

Think, Alona, think! Talking her out of it was never going to happen. I couldn't run. Hiding was definitely out, duh. So, I did the only thing I could.

I screamed bloody murder... because I had a feeling that was exactly where this was headed.

❦ 15 ❦

Will

I didn't bother with waiting for the elevator, just plowed through the lobby to the emergency stairs and up to the fifth floor, taking the steps two at a time. I cursed myself for leaving my phone in the car. At the very least, I could have called and tried to warn Alona while I was running, but it was like I'd stopped thinking the second I'd heard Mina was at the hospital.

I yanked open the door and burst into the hallway on the fifth floor, startling a nurse who happened to be passing by at the same time.

"Can I help you?" she asked, annoyed.

I ignored her and charged past the nurses' station and down the corridor toward Lily's room. The door was open, I could see that much, but I couldn't hear her, as I had before.

Dread filled me, but I forced it back with an attempt at logic. *She might be sleeping. Or, maybe they took her for more tests.*

I jogged toward the door, moving slower than I had before, almost afraid to look inside.

And when I did, I saw exactly what I'd expected and feared. Lily's bed empty, the covers shoved back. My heart sank.

Mrs. Turner looked up from her paperback, startled. "Will? Did you forget something?"

"Where is Al . . . Lily?" I shifted my weight from foot to foot, feeling potentially vital seconds tick away.

She frowned. "Physical therapy. Is something wrong? You look panicked."

Physical therapy. That actually sounded legitimate. What were the chances that it was? Could I have beaten Mina and John here?

"She'll probably be back in an hour, I'd guess." She looked thoughtful. "Actually, the orderly never said how long it would take."

Instinct whispered to me, telling me something was off. "Was she scheduled for therapy this morning?" I asked. "She didn't mention it to me earlier."

Mrs. Turner put down her book. "You know, we didn't know anything about it, either, but I think they're getting her ready to go home." She gave me a weary but hopeful smile.

No. The Order was here somewhere. And they had Alona.

But had they taken her from the hospital, or were they still here with her somewhere?

It would be risky to take her from the hospital, because even if they managed to remove Alona, they still had Lily to deal with. They'd have to get her back here somehow. So, it wasn't just sneaking her out, but sneaking her back in as well.

It might be easier to find an isolated place within the hospital instead. But where?

"Did you go with to get her set up?" I asked.

"No, the orderly recommended that she go alone, and that's what she wanted, too," Mrs. Turner said. "It's been hard for her, I think, adjusting to these new circumstances."

"More than you know," I muttered.

"What?"

"Nothing," I said. So, either Mina and John were going to attempt to hijack her somewhere between her room and physical therapy . . . or the orderly was in on it. I remembered suddenly Lucy saying the hospital chaplain was involved. He, of all people, would probably know the hospital personnel well enough to find a true believer or someone willing to look the other way for a little extra green.

"Are you sure you're okay?" she asked again. "You just seem . . . out of sorts." She offered me a kind smile, so similar to Lily's, and patted the bed. "You want to sit down and tell me about it?"

I swallowed a hysterical laugh I could feel bubbling in the back of my throat. *Well, you see Mrs. Turner, your daughter is not actually your daughter, at least not right now.*

I shook my head. "Thanks, but I'm okay."

"You're welcome to wait here for her, if you want. But I don't know what kind of shape she'll be in when she gets back."

You could say that again.

"I know things have been tough," she continued, "but your friendship means the world to her. You should have seen the way she lit up earlier when you walked in." Mrs. Turner gave me a significant look.

Alona. My chest ached with the need to find her. If I didn't find and stop them in time, and she was ... boxed, then our last conversation would be the one we had this morning. No, I couldn't let that happen.

"I know things have been tough between the two of you, but I hope you can figure it out."

Me, too. "Mrs. Turner, do you remember anything about the orderly that picked up ... Lily?"

She frowned at me. "Why?"

Oh, good question, one for which I didn't have an answer. I thought quickly, trying to come up with something that would seem legit without causing a panic. The last thing I wanted was the entire hospital in an uproar. That might cause Mina to try to hurry, or worse yet, take Alona and Lily out of here, assuming they were here to begin with. "I was just wondering if it was the same guy I saw on the elevator this morning with a patient," I lied. "He's a diner regular, I think."

"Oh." She looked faintly confused. "I don't know. He was tall with dreadlocks. But I didn't catch his name."

Crap.

She brightened. "His scrubs were adorable. They were dark blue with balloons and teddy bears in party hats on them."

Yeah. *That* was helpful. Then I realized she was waiting for a response. "Oh, yeah, that sounds like him," I said quickly. "Nice guy."

She nodded again, still seeming baffled by the turn of our conversation.

"I'm just going to go walk around a little, stretch my legs, check things out, while I'm waiting for Lily." Like I hadn't already spent way too much time in this hospital. But right now, the only solid lead I had was the priest. I could probably track down his office easily enough, assuming he was there and not with Mina and John. He'd been the one to call them in, so I had a hard time imagining him sitting idly by, doing paperwork or something, while they worked to remove this—what had Lucy called it?—manifestation.

"Okay," Mrs. Turner said, "but don't get in the way or bother people while they're supposed to be working." She pointed a finger at me.

"Got it." I spun on my heel and started back the way I'd come. I didn't know the priest's name, but I bet someone at the nurses' station could direct me to the chaplain's office. If

I had to, I'd page him and make him come to me. From there, I'd have to figure out what to say, another lie, but at least I'd be headed in the right direction.

At the nurses' station, a mother with three children clinging to her legs had the attention of both nurses as she expressed displeasure about something to do with a fourth kid and a lack of Jell-O on his lunch tray yesterday.

Come on, come on.

"Can I help you?" One of the nurses finally turned her attention to me. It was the same one who'd looked at me disapprovingly when I'd burst in from the stairs, and she didn't seem any happier with me now.

"I'm looking for the—" A flash of color, red on a dark blue background, passed by at the edge of my vision.

I turned quickly to see a tall man with short dreadlocks moving down the opposite branch of the hall, pushing a gurney ahead of him. His scrub shirt was dark blue with teddy bears in party hats and red balloons printed all over them.

Yes! My heart picked up an extra beat in the rush of adrenaline. This had to be him, right? The orderly who'd taken Alona to wherever she was.

"Young man?" the nurse asked, her mouth pursed tightly.

"Never mind," I said quickly, and chased after the orderly. "Hey, wait, stop."

He froze and then turned to give me a wary look over his shoulder.

Yeah, this was the guy.

"Listen." I moved a little closer. "I got separated from the others, but I'm supposed to be helping."

He shook his head, his eyes still watchful. "I don't know what you're talking about. I got to get back to work, though, so—"

"The situation with room 512 and the Order," I said in a voice just above a whisper. If I was wrong, and he had no idea what I was talking about, I was going to resemble a serious brand of crazy.

But recognition flashed over his expression. "Yeah. Yeah, okay." He leaned toward me. "They're downstairs."

I felt a huge rush of relief. They were still in the hospital. "Where?" I asked, trying not to sound desperate and like I was ready to shake him for the information.

I must have only partially succeeded, though, because he pulled back slightly to frown at me.

"I'm going to be in so much trouble for being late. I'm supposed to be training, but I screwed up the time, and then I couldn't find my notes on where we were supposed to meet, and you know how the Order is about punctuality." I could hear myself rambling, saying too much, anything I thought might open the door to the information he held that I needed.

"It's all right," he said, his hands out as if to calm me. "We'll get you there. Just take the elevator to the basement. Turn right into the hall, and then left down the first hall. First door with no windows."

Yeah, that didn't sound ominous at all. "Thanks, man,

I really appreciate it." The relief in my voice, at least, was genuine.

"You better hurry, though," he said. "Father Hayes said it wouldn't take very long. And I gotta be down there in a little while to pick her up and bring her back."

I couldn't help but wonder how much he knew, what he would think when he went to pick up Lily from that windowless space and found her an empty shell once more. Was he expecting it? Or would it give him second thoughts about his involvement in something he probably didn't completely understand?

Either way, I didn't want to wait around to find out.

I nodded my thanks at him and took off for the elevator.

❧ 16 ❧

Alona

Father Hayes looked alarmed. "Someone will hear her screaming, even down here."

Good. I took another deep breath and continued at the top of my lungs, even though my voice had already faded into something less of a scream and more of an annoying screech.

Mina seemed flustered, caught between keeping the disruptor aimed at me and moving faster to get the boxes laid out. "Just help me," she ordered the priest. "Put the boxes on the floor and—"

Behind me, I heard the door open abruptly. Both Mina and the priest jumped. "What the hell are you doing?" a man's voice demanded.

Yes! I was saved. I tried to crane around to see him but could only catch a glimpse of jeans and the cuff of a faded flannel shirt. "They kidnapped me," I said, my voice croaking. "Call the police."

"You're going to have half the hospital down here, Mina," he said, clearly irritated.

My heart fell. The man, my potential rescuer, was evidently part of Mina's crew.

A second later, hands shoved rough fabric smelling heavily of bleach and laundry detergent into my mouth, pulling it tight and tying it off at the back of my head, catching some of my hair painfully in the process. The material sucked all the moisture out of my mouth, and it tasted horrible.

"If you're going to survive as a full member, your planning skills need improvement," he said, sounding reproving.

I was only half-listening, focused more on trying to get the gag to loosen. He'd pulled it so tight I couldn't even bite down on it. Not that I even had a chance in hell of chewing through it in hours, which was way more time than it would take for them to do what they were going to do.

"I would have had it," she said plaintively. "I just needed a few more seconds."

He made a sound of disgust, and she flinched a little. That caught my attention. Whoever this guy was, Mina was afraid of him.

"Get on with it," he said. "Or do you need me to do that, too?"

She shook her head rapidly, her hair flying around her pinched white face.

With Mina's guidance, the priest finished laying out the boxes and connecting the individual cords to one larger one that lay on the floor near an available wall outlet, and then Mina moved to stand at my side. She brought the disruptor closer, pressing it hard against my shoulder. The wires on the open end dug into my skin through the hospital gown.

I squirmed in my chair, but my lower half was still astonishingly uncooperative. There was no way I would be getting out of here under my own power, even if I could somehow get past the three of them. I screamed against the gag, but the muffled sound that emerged would never travel past the closed door. So . . . this was it.

My heart was beating a thousand times a minute, shaking me with it. I wondered if it hurt to be boxed, or if I just wouldn't feel anything more. Tears trickled down my face to be absorbed by the fabric around my mouth.

Will. I wanted him here so badly. I mean, if this was it, then at least I wouldn't be alone.

"Ready?" Mina asked.

The priest nodded anxiously, his face covered in a light sheen of sweat.

"It's your show," the man behind me said, sounding impatient.

She took a deep breath and pressed buttons on her device.

A faint blue glow emerged, and electricity ran through me, clamping my jaws shut and arching my back. The pain felt like fire over my whole body. Agonized whimpers escaped my mouth despite my best efforts.

Then the strangest sensation suffused me, a separating, one becoming two, like peeling the backing from a sticker or removing that layer of dead sunburned skin. I could feel myself, distinct once more, within Lily.

Mina skimmed her free hand over the surface of my arm. My actual arm, not Lily's. Staring down at myself, I could see the ghostly—no pun intended—outline of my own body overlaid on Lily's. I might have cried with relief except I knew this meant I was likely one step closer to those damn boxes on the floor.

I struggled to pull myself free of Lily's body, but it held me as securely as a mouse on one of those nasty glue traps my step-Mothra had insisted on using in the garage at their house.

"Get ready, or you're going to lose it," the man behind me said, but he made no move to help her. "It's going to fight you."

It? Oh, hell no. And you bet your life I was going to fight.

Mina nodded, but didn't look up. Her hand hovered above my wrist, just barely making contact, and the next time I lurched upward in an attempt to free myself, her fingers closed around my arm.

I watched in astonishment as she set her feet on the floor, bracing herself, and began to tug at me with one hand—none too gently, I might add—while using the other to keep the end of the disruptor pressed against the shoulder where Lily and I were still joined.

In a few seconds, she'd pulled me out from the waist up. I could see my white shirt with the treadmark again, and my long blond hair brushed against my cheek. I was almost free! It felt strange after so many hours as Lily.

"Look, it was an accident," I said quickly, twisting my wrist in Mina's grasp, trying to break free. "I'm out now. I promise I'm not going back in. Trust me." I was sweaty with panic. I couldn't run. I was still merged with Lily's body from the waist down,

"Transition, Mina. Switch over, or you're going to lose it," the man ordered.

Behind me, I sensed movement and looked to see Lily slumping against the side of her chair. Oh, God. I flashed back to the memory of Mrs. Turner holding me/Lily against her shoulder. She would be destroyed to see her daughter like this. My heart ached for the girl who would never wake up to see the flowers her father had brought her, the way her mother took care of her, and even her brother returning something to her that he knew she would want.

The priest was staring at Lily and looked sickened. "Is this normal?" he asked. The priest had a point. Lily didn't look good, and I didn't think it wasn't just the absence of vitality and movement. Actually, she seemed worse than before. She was paler, her skin grayer.

The man in the flannel shirt shook his head grimly. I could see more of him now. He had wiry dark hair that looked like it would be curly if he let it grow. His face was hard with deep lines carved in his forehead and on either side of his mouth, like he worked outside or had lots of stress. "They must have bonded. If the entity is embedded long enough, the host becomes dependent on the entity's energy. And the entity—"

Everyone shifted their gazes to me.

"—becomes dependent on the host, feeding on the electrical energy provided by the body. It's a cycle."

I looked down at myself and saw that my arms were disappearing. I gasped. They weren't flickering, not like all the times before, just slowly vanishing like they'd never been there. And I didn't feel a thing.

Behind me, Lily began gasping for air, a horrible thick sound. She was dying, I was disappearing, and it was all my fault.

"Hurry up," he snapped at Mina. "The possession drained it. If it disappears now, it'll be gone for good. The Order wants a chance to study it first," the flannel-shirt guy said.

Study me? Why? For how long? Would I be caged up or in pieces? My throat closed with fear. I wanted to struggle, but I had no means for it. I couldn't even push myself away.

Mina fumbled with the disruptor, moving it up to my neck. "I'm working on it," she snapped to the guy behind me, who seemed to be a boss of some kind. "Can you just let me do this?"

She bent down and plugged the giant cord into the wall. Instantly, the boxes on the floor began to glow with a sickly yellow light that spilled out of a thin crack along the tops. Then the tops began to retract, and that awful parody of the white light began to seep out toward me, like long creepy fingers reaching.

I screamed, but no one even flinched.

In the midst of this chaos, the door burst open once more. As one, everyone, except Lily, turned to look.

As if my desperation had summoned him like a homing beacon, Will Killian stood in the doorway, out of breath, normally pale cheeks flushed with color.

The guy in flannel smiled. "Will," he said, sounding pleased. "What are you doing—"

Will ignored him. "Stop," he shouted at Mina. "Turn it off." He rushed forward and shoved at her, knocking her hand away from me, sending the disruptor flying across the room toward the priest.

But it was too late. I could feel the light from those boxes pulling me in, each one a slightly different sensation. Some prickly like pins, some hot like the blistering heat rising from fresh asphalt, all painful. It was sectioning me into pieces.

In that second, everything slowed down, becoming very quiet and clear.

I could let the boxes take me in and pull me apart, and the Order would study me, whatever hellish ordeal that might involve.

I could just let myself go. Just be gone. It wouldn't be so bad, would it? Being nothing would be nothing . . . right?

Or, I could try. Lily's body would protect me from the boxes. That's why they'd had to use the disruptor in the first place. But to voluntarily return to her dying body, knowing

I'd be stuck? I felt sick at just the idea. That would make me what Will had accused me of being, a body snatcher, and not even of a body I wanted. I couldn't be Lily Turner.

But if flannel guy was right about Lily and me being dependent on each other, she might survive with my help. She might live because of me. There had to be a reason I'd been sent back from the light, right? Maybe this was it. Maybe we could save each other. And if we lived through this, there might be another chance for us. An opportunity for Lily to keep living and me to be me again, right? But if I didn't take this chance now, we were both done for. And I couldn't just let her die, not when I'd caused this to happen and might be able to stop it. . . .

In my mind, I saw Mrs. Turner's tear-stained face before me again, the moment she realized her daughter was awake. *I knew you would come back. I knew there was a reason to keep hoping.*

I turned my head and met Will's gaze. Eyes wide, he shook his head at me as though he could hear what I was thinking.

I'm sorry. Then I wrenched myself backward toward Lily, praying Mrs. Turner had been right.

❧ 17 ❧

Will

"**N**o!" I shouted. But Alona was gone.

The boxes remained open and glowing, though, and none of the others in the closet seemed sure where to look. But I knew. I knew Alona. Self-preservation was never very far down on that girl's list.

I stared down at Lily. She appeared no different, still struggling to breathe and so pale she might as well have been translucent. But I was almost positive that's where Alona had gone. She'd taken Lily to use for her own purposes again, and this time, it might kill Lily.

Damn it.

But oddly enough, that last look she'd given me had not been one of triumph. Not at all. She'd seemed sad, desperate maybe, and . . . resigned, if I had to describe it.

"Did it fade out?" Mina asked.

John stepped forward around both of us to unplug the main box cord from the wall. "It's possible. But there's only one way to know for sure. We'll wait." He nodded at Lily. "The girl is dying anyway."

I froze. "What?"

"The entity was in place for so long, she won't survive without it," he said. "But even if the entity managed to repossess her, it's severely depleted. Removing it won't be an issue, especially once the girl dies."

Thoughts whirled around in my head, making it difficult for me to catch hold of one.

Lily was dying? Had Alona known that? Had she figured out that Lily would not survive without her? That would have explained the expression on her face right before she disappeared.

Had Alona just attempted to save Lily's life?

The very idea stirred up more thoughts I couldn't quite pin down.

Granted, trying to save Lily by reclaiming her would have benefits for Alona, too, like not being boxed, but she had to have known that being permanently stuck in Lily was a possibility. And yet she'd tried anyway.

"We should relocate. Someone may have heard the ruckus." John reached for the handles of Lily's wheelchair.

I moved to block him. "No."

He looked at me, startled.

"You say you're concerned about the living, but the dead were the living once. You don't get to ignore that just because it's more convenient for your philosophy and helps you sleep better at night," I said.

John blanched.

"Yeah, listen to the new recruit," Mina said softly. "The one you're all fighting over."

I ignored her. "If the spirit even survived, if Alona survived," I deliberately used her name, watching John's eyebrows shoot skyward, "I'm sure as hell not going to just sit here and watch Lily die so you can get to Alona that much faster." I reached down and carefully peeled the gag away from her mouth. Lily's mouth was red and raw on the edges from where Alona had been screaming.

"A Killian rides to the rescue again. All the poor dead people who need your help." A weary bitterness settled across John's face. "It's supposed to be about the greater good, Will. Your father never understood that, either."

"He did," I snapped. "His definition of good was just a little broader than yours, I think."

I grabbed Lily's wheelchair and started to pull it away, pausing only to open the door behind me.

"She's possessed," John spat at me.

"You don't know that."

"It's an abomination," he continued.

"And you don't get to decide that." The light had sent Alona back, and if one held with the belief that the light was representative of some all-knowing, all-powerful force, then the light had been aware of this outcome all along and done nothing to stop it. In fact, by sending her back, it might have very well created the events leading to this moment. I didn't know, and I couldn't judge. And I wouldn't allow John and the Order to judge, either.

"You'll be calling us, begging for help before you know it," he said with disgust.

Maybe, but at least I'd know the price for their help next time, and it was far too high.

"Don't." Mina stepped forward, her hand closing around my wrist tightly. "If she's still possessed, I need this, Will." Her eyes pleaded with me, showing her desperation more plainly than words ever could.

"You are never going to be good enough," I said to her, and she flinched. "No one is ever good enough for him because he doesn't feel good enough himself, always comparing you to other people, just like he compared himself to my dad."

John made a disgusted noise. "You don't know what you're talking about."

I didn't, not for sure, but based on what Mina had said and his reaction to my words just now, I felt it was a fairly good guess. "So you have to be who you are, whoever that is," I said to Mina. "Call Lucy and tell her the truth."

She jerked back, her gaze skating immediately to her father for his reaction. It wasn't good. His face reddened, and he glared at her, before turning his attention to me.

"If you're implying that anything in my division is not running as it should—" he blustered.

"Not your division, your family. And you know it's not," I said. "Call Lucy," I said to Mina again.

This time, she nodded, a tiny motion, almost imperceptible, but still there.

I pulled Lily's chair out into the hall. To my surprise, the priest followed us. I watched him warily as I turned the chair around and aimed it for the elevators, but he made no attempt to stop me.

"I was trying to save the girl," he said quietly.

"I know, Father." *Me, too. Both of them.*

"I didn't know that they would hurt her and—"

The wheelchair jerked in my hands.

I looked down. Lily's whole body was shaking so hard the chair rattled, and her face had turned an ominous shade of blue.

Fear froze me in place. Whatever Alona had done, it was not enough. Lily was dying, and now she would take Alona with her. I would lose both of them.

"Help, someone! We need help!" The priest took off down the hall shouting.

I followed, one hand on Lily's slumped shoulder and the other on the chair, moving as fast as I dared. "It's okay. It's going to be okay." I just kept repeating the words, praying I wouldn't hear a final gasp from her. I'd grown used to the idea of life without Lily. But Alona? What would I do without her? No matter how much she drove me crazy sometimes, I needed that—I needed her—in my life.

Several people in scrubs came running toward us. The priest had done his job.

"What happened?"

"What did you see?"

"What is she being treated for?"

They were all calling questions to me in calm but urgent voices that unnerved me. "I just found her this way," I said in answer to all of them. The truth, but lame. I was pretty sure they didn't believe me, especially when they saw the gag down around her neck.

They shoved me away from her and lowered her to the floor.

Two of them started CPR, while a third ran for a phone farther down the hall.

In what seemed like seconds, the entire hall was filled with medical personnel, a crash cart ... and Mrs. Turner.

She took one look at Lily on the floor and launched herself at me. "What did you do? What did you do to my baby?" Each word came with a punch.

I tried to avoid most of them, but some landed, each one with the fury born of a mother protecting her child.

"You stay away! Stay away from her!" Mrs. Turner shoved at me, and I let her.

They loaded Lily up on a gurney and raced away. Mrs. Turner followed them at a run.

And I ... I could do nothing but watch and wait.

❦ 18 ❦

Will

Three days later, and still, they wouldn't let me see her. I knew the Turners had taken her home from the hospital yesterday afternoon, thanks to a brief and guarded update from Father Hayes, the hospital chaplain. I'd called and begged him for information.

She was continuing to recover was all he'd say, which told me absolutely nothing of what I needed to know. Was Alona still there? If she was, was she okay? Could she communicate? Or was she now trapped inside the girl she'd tried to save?

I'd tried to call their house twice yesterday. The first time, Mrs. Turner had simply hung up on me. The second time, she'd threatened to call the police. She still held me responsible for what had happened to Lily in the hospital. I couldn't exactly blame her. The story I'd given—that I'd been looking for a vending machine and happened to stumble across Lily, unconscious in her chair—was weak at best. But since telling the truth was out of the question, I was sort of stuck with the lies I'd told on the fly that day.

Those same lies, though, were now keeping me from Alona—*if* she was still here.

The not-knowing was killing me.

"You're pacing again," my mother said, looking up at me with exasperation from where she was mixing batter in a bowl on the kitchen counter.

"Sorry," I said, but I didn't stop. Eight steps to the back door, eight steps to the doorway to the hall, back and forth. It was kind of soothing, in an annoying, repetitive kind of way.

"Will, you need to give them a little bit of time to adjust. Dealing with a sick child is very stressful," she said. "I'm sure Mrs. Turner doesn't really blame you for anything." She expertly scraped the bowl into the brownie pan without so much as a single drop of batter hitting the counter. She was making a batch of brownies this afternoon to drop off at the Turners' house tomorrow, assuming they even let her reach the front door. I wasn't sure if Mrs. Turner's anger with me would spill over to my mom or not. I hoped not.

Unfortunately, I'd had to give my mom the same weak-ass story as everyone else. Because explaining about the Order was kind of tied up in explaining about my dad, and I didn't think it was my place to do so. Knowing he'd kept even more stuff from her than she'd originally thought would only make her feel worse. And telling her about Alona potentially inhabiting Lily's body was definitely out of the question.

I raked my hands through my hair. "But if I could just talk to her, then I'd know for sure that she's okay." *She*, of course, meant Lily to my mom and Alona to me.

What troubled me most was that Alona had made no attempt to contact me. Which meant what? I had no idea, but I could think of endless bad news scenarios. Like maybe she'd vanished after all, or maybe Lily had slipped back into a coma and buried Alona down under all those of layers of unconsciousness. Maybe Alona was angry with me for all the things I'd said to her earlier that day, when we were alone in Lily's hospital room. Or maybe she thought I was angry with her, as I had been in those last few minutes before I realized she was trying to save Lily, not just herself.

God, thinking of all the possible ways this could be messed up made my stomach hurt.

"Just relax. Let things cool off for a bit. Concentrate on your other friends and work, and eventually things will calm down." She bent down, opened the oven door, and slid the pan of brownies in.

Eventually? Like I could just, what, forget about the fact that I had no idea whether this girl I cared so much about still existed or not?

"Oh, that reminds me. Sam thought one of your tires looked a little low, so I gave him your keys in case he needed to put on the spare," she said, closing the oven and setting the timer.

I nodded, my mind still focused on Alona and Lily.

"He says you have three full garbage bags in the trunk," she continued. "Why on earth are you driving around with garbage in your trunk?"

Garbage? It took a second for the memory to drop into place. The bags I'd swiped from the foot of Alona's driveway before everything had gotten so complicated. Bags that would hopefully contain one or more treasured items from her life.

I stopped pacing. If Alona was still present inside Lily, and if I could find something meaningful in those bags of trash, that would be a better present than any brownies, no matter how good my mom's recipe was. It might even convince her, if need be, to take a stand against Mrs. Turner and insist on seeing me. Of course, that was assuming I could get close enough to Alona/Lily to show her what I'd found.

No. I shook my head. I'd worry about that part after I'd figured out if I'd grabbed anything worth saving.

I stalked to the back door, my steps now filled with purpose.

"Where are you going?" my mom asked.

"To clean up a mess," I said.

❦ 19 ❧

Alona

"Are you sure you're ready for this?" Mrs. Turner asked, as we stood at the top of the stairs.

I nodded.

She took my one hand and locked it around the wooden stair railing and then wrapped my other hand inside her own.

"Just take it slowly," she cautioned. "If you get too tired, we can stop."

But I knew I wouldn't stop. I'd slept on the couch last night in their living room and it had been miserable for multiple reasons.

First, the Turners might have love, but they didn't have money. Or at least not enough for a new couch that didn't sag toward the back, threatening to swallow me up. Second, no privacy. I didn't mind Mrs. Turner getting up to check on me in the night. However, waking up to find Tyler two inches from my face, where he was apparently making sure I was still breathing, was another experience all together. Third, the voices.

The doctors had mentioned all kinds of possible side effects, most of them still from the original car accident injuries but some from that brief period when Lily's . . . my heart had stopped. Dizziness, frequent headaches, disorientation, muscle aches, etc.

Nobody had said anything about hearing voices, though. It had started in the hospital. But honestly, I hadn't paid much attention to it. In the hospital, there's a constant low level of noise, including voices from down the hall, next door, and so on.

At the Turner house, though, it was unavoidable. I'd heard them yesterday for the first time. Voices whispering, sometimes barely audible, other times as clear as if someone were right next to my ear. But no one ever was.

And at one point yesterday, when I'd sat down in the fat and faded recliner in the corner of the living room, an old lady voice, cracked with age, had shrieked at me to get up.

When I'd jumped up—or as close as I could come to it with my ugly metal hospital-issue cane and my still damaged legs, which was more like a slow and ugly lurch forward— Mrs. Turner had asked me what was wrong.

Too tired and shaken to make something up, I'd just said

that I didn't feel like I should sit there, that the chair seemed to belong to someone else.

Instead of being freaked out, though, as I'd expected, Mrs. Turner had beamed at me. The chair had apparently belonged to Granny Simmy—Grandma Simone—and it had been one of the few pieces of furniture she'd ever bought new, and she'd treasured it for years while she was still alive, never letting any of the grandchildren sit in it.

Mrs. Turner thought I was just remembering. I wasn't sure what was happening to me.

I was hoping that downstairs might provide a little more peace and quiet, or at least fewer people to stare at me when I was listening to something they couldn't hear.

We inched our way down the stairs to the basement, where Lily's room was. Tyler and the Turners had bedrooms upstairs, but they'd set up Lily in the basement to give her "space."

At the bottom, I found myself in a small family room with a big, boxy television on a stand, another saggy couch— this one even worse than the one upstairs—and lots and lots of shag carpeting. Gag.

Mrs. Turner led me through the family room and down a narrow hall that held two doors directly across from one another.

"Here we are," she said, opening the left-hand door.

The room itself was painted a bright and simple white. A good thing, too, because the carpeting was an eye-blinding pink. Any kind of pattern or paint color on the wall probably would have caused heads to spontaneously combust. As it was, the torn-out magazine pictures of celebrities spread out all over in various minicollages on the wall were bad enough. A worn and battered twin bed stood to my right. The pale pink comforter with carriages, castles, and fairies was a match to the sheet I remembered from the hospital room.

A mismatched desk and dresser dominated the opposite wall, and then two big closets took up the far end. Three large windows ran along the length of the wall with the desk and dresser. The house was built into a hill, so the windows were almost like the ones upstairs instead of the cramped tiny basement windows set high in the walls, like at my house.

"See? We didn't change anything," Mrs. Turner said proudly.

I nodded. Of course, it didn't look the least bit familiar to me, except for glimpses of what I'd seen a couple of months ago in a photograph of Will, Lily, and Joonie in this room last year some time.

"It's great," I said. Couldn't help but notice there was no phone in the room, though. I wondered if it had always been that way or if she'd removed it specifically because of my arrival.

Mrs. Turner had refused to give me back my cell phone after "the incident" at the hospital. That's what we were calling it. The incident. She blamed Will for what had happened, even though it was obvious she wasn't entirely sure *what* had happened. Only that he'd been there, somehow involved, and it must therefore be his fault, mainly because she didn't have anyone else to blame it on.

I'd have pushed harder to talk with him, but he'd made no effort to reach me, as far as I knew, and I figured he might still be mad. I hadn't had a chance to explain to him what I was doing in taking over Lily's body. He probably thought I'd done it just because I could. And if that was the case, he might never talk to me again. My heart ached at the idea that I was in this alone now. I missed him.

"Are you all right, honey?" Mrs. Turner asked. "You look pale."

"Just tired, I guess." In truth, I was bone-weary exhausted. This being alive was much more work than I remembered it being. Of course, seeing as I was in a damaged body, one that wasn't my own, maybe it wasn't all that surprising that it took more effort than I remembered.

"Why don't you lie down for a couple of hours? Dinner won't be ready until about six anyway," Mrs. Turner said.

Planting face first into the pillow and shutting out the world for a while sounded like a wonderful idea.

I let Mrs. Turner pull back the covers and help me into bed. I could probably have managed it myself, but it was kind of nice to have the assistance.

She pulled the sheet up to my shoulder and tucked it around me. "And Blankie's under your pillow again," she whispered before kissing my forehead and backing away.

She left the room and closed the door partially behind

her. With an effort, I rolled onto my side and slid my hand under the pillow, locating the ragged bit of satin that was Lily's Blankie with my fingertips. Even the idea of how many germs it might hold didn't stop me from touching it. How many nights had she laid here, just like this, thinking and wondering about tomorrow? How long would I be here doing that in her stead?

Thinking of all this, I started to doze off, and that's when the voices started . . . again.

"This is her?" The first one asked. The speaker sounded female and young. I kept my eyes squinched shut. *There's no one there. No one. No one. No one . . .*

"I guess," the second voice, male, this time, said.

"I don't get what the big deal is," the female said, sounding impatient. "So, she's awake. I don't understand why he can't help us because of *her*."

What was worse, this time these voices sounded somehow familiar. Great. I was making friends with these figments of my brain-damaged imagination.

"I mean, first Alona disappears without so much as a word," she continued.

My eyes snapped open. I still couldn't see anything, but the voices sounded like they were coming from the foot of my bed.

"Then Will gets in his head that this girl is more important than helping us move on to the light. This thing with Claire and Todd is not going to last forever. I hope he knows that."

"Liesel?" I asked incredulously, pushing myself up into a sitting position.

A shocked silence filled the room and held for a full second.

"She can see us? Wait, you can see us?" Her voice moved closer, and I instinctively moved back.

"No," I admitted. "But I can hear you."

"You're another ghost-talker?" She asked in disbelief. "Just like Will?"

I opened my mouth to explain who I was, but then stopped. If I told them I was Alona and I'd managed to take over a body, word would spread and quickly. Would there be hundreds of ghosts lined up at the hospital to try this out on the next poor, unsuspecting coma patient? I wasn't sure it would work since I didn't entirely understand why it had worked for me. But neither did I like the idea of them trying.

"Yeah, I guess," I managed to say.

"How did you know my name?" Liesel demanded.

"Why can't you see us?" Eric asked.

I answered the easier question, Eric's, first, hoping they might take my answer for both. "I have no idea," I admitted. In theory, I shouldn't have been able to see or hear them, but as a ghost, I'd been able to do both easily. Maybe being able to hear them was just some kind of side effect from the merging of Lily and me.

"Okay, so listen, I have this friend Claire," Liesel began.

I groaned inwardly, imagining yet another recitation of the sordid tale of Liesel, Eric, and Claire.

A light tapping sounded at the far window.

I looked over to see Will, his hands cupped to the glass to peer inside. My heart did somersaults in my chest. He was here! He couldn't be too angry at me, then, could he?

"Quick, move!" Liesel ordered Eric. "If he sees us here, he'll kill us all over again."

I didn't hear anything more, and then the faint sound of whispering came from the hall beyond my room. Clearly, they'd fled for the moment.

I pulled the covers off myself, fumbling with them a little and grateful I'd stayed dressed in Lily's best jeans and T-shirt, which wasn't saying much, and started for the window. The moment Will saw me, his face relaxed and he smiled, an event so rare that it stopped me in my tracks and made my pulse accelerate.

No, he wasn't angry at all, it seemed. Of course, that might end up being the least of our problems. How did we go about this? We were friends still? More? And were we friends as Alona and Will? Or as Lily and Will? Would he ever be able to see me for who I was, when I looked like someone else?

Just thinking about it made my head, and heart, hurt.

❧ 20 ❧

Will

Lily—well, Alona, really, I guess—came to the window slowly, limping as she walked and her hands out at her sides as if to catch herself if she started to fall.

She struggled to raise the window one-handed, hanging on to the sill with her other hand for balance. I wanted to help, but the screen was down so I couldn't reach it. Plus, I could read a very familiar stubbornness on her face, though it was not an expression I was accustomed to seeing on this particular face.

She finally managed to shove the window up and prop her hand under it to keep it from falling.

"Hi," I said, feeling awkward and shy suddenly, like this wasn't the girl I'd been making out with in the bushes just a few days ago. I mean, it was, but it also wasn't.

"Hi," she said back, in an equally uncomfortable tone. Her gaze darted everywhere but my face.

I hesitated. "I guess I just wanted to be sure that you're okay after everything that happened with the Order and—"

"Liesel and Eric are here," she said brightly in warning. "They're asking for my help."

"What?" I asked, confused.

Liesel burst in from the hallway with Eric at her heels. "You weren't supposed to tell him!" she protested. "We just came to see who was taking up all of your time instead of us," Liesel said to me with a pout. "And then it turns out she's a ghost-talker like you."

I stared at Lily/Alona.

"I can hear them, but I can't see them," she said to me in an undertone.

But that shouldn't have been possible. Lily had never been able to see or hear ghosts before, nor had Alona when she was alive, I was fairly certain. Then again, Lily had almost died while Alona was merged with her. Who knew what the combination of a near-death experience and a ghost living inside of you would do?

"So, now that there's two of you, you can really step it up." Liesel smoothed her hands down the front of her dress. "I'm thinking that if we talk with Claire tomorrow—"

I sighed. "Eric, man, you've got to speak up."

He glared at me. "Shut up, Will."

Alona/Lily looked intrigued.

"What does Eric have to do with any of this?" Liesel asked, sounding confused.

"In a word? Everything," I said.

Eric's face was turning red, and he shoved his hair back from his eyes. "You said I could pick my moment," he said to me.

"Dude, you've had more than thirty years," I said. "That's a lot of moments."

"Oh," Alona/Lily said suddenly. "He's in love with Liesel."

Clearly, this merging had not affected Alona's mad observation skills. I'd had to have Eric tell me, but she'd pieced it together on her own.

"What?" Liesel shrieked, staring at Eric as if she'd never seen him before.

Eric looked around like he was desperate for escape, but I nodded at him, encouraging.

He coughed, cleared his throat, and then stuffed his hands in the pockets of his powder-blue tux pants. "So, yeah." He swallowed hard. "I'm in love with you, Liesel. I have been since the day we died." He paused, shifting his weight nervously. "Actually, before that even," he added, stammering a little.

"I know that you feel guilty, like we betrayed Claire," he said. "But the truth is, I never felt that way about her. Not ever." He reached out and took her hand, turning her to face him. "I swear, I didn't even know she liked me until after . . . well, after." He blushed.

261

"So, what I'm trying to say is," he continued, "you might have other reasons for staying here in the in-between, but I stayed, and am *staying*, because of you."

"Oh." I couldn't see Liesel's expression with her back to me, but it sounded like she was crying. "I love you, too," she said, sniffling. "I just felt so bad because I thought you and Claire—"

"No, never. It's always been you."

Then they were kissing each other, with very enthusiastic amounts of tongue, I couldn't help noticing.

I grimaced and looked away.

"What are they doing?" Alona/Lily whispered.

"Slobbering on each other, mostly."

She crinkled up her nose in disgust and rolled her eyes at me, which made me laugh. She was still Alona, though maybe a slightly different version. Alona 2.0 or something.

I felt the light before I saw it, the warmth that was somehow . . . more than anything. It came from above, moving like liquid sunshine, bringing with it that feeling of some unknowable knot on your insides finally relaxing.

It enveloped Liesel and Eric as they were kissing. They didn't even seem to notice.

Alona/Lily turned slightly to stare in their general direction with undisguised longing and envy. "It's here, isn't it? The light?" she asked quietly.

"Yeah," I said, startled. "You can see it?"

She shook her head. "I can feel it, sort of. Just a change in the room. A warmth." A tear rolled down her cheek, but I wasn't sure if she noticed.

The light grew stronger then, the two of them becoming the blindingly bright center until it was so intense, I had to look away.

Then the light began to fade, taking Liesel and Eric with it.

I blinked rapidly, a bright afterimage of the two of them temporarily burned into my vision.

"You okay?" I asked.

She nodded and wiped her face with her hand.

"We'll find a way to fix this," I said, striving to sound confident. "A way for you to go on to the light if you want, and for Lily to stay and still be okay."

She didn't look so sure about that, and to be honest, neither was I.

"In the meantime, though, I have something for you." I bent down and picked up the shoe box I'd brought over.

With a small amount of struggle, she managed to raise the screen.

I handed the box in to her, my fingers brushing hers in the process, and an odd, almost electric, jolt shot through me. It made me want to wrap her hand in mine and hold on. But I resisted.

She looked at the shoe box and then me. "Those are men's shoes," she pointed out. "And if this picture is accurate, they're ugly, too. I mean, tassels, really?"

Ah, some things never change.

"Not that I don't appreciate the thought," she added

quickly, though it was clear any thought that involved bringing her ugly men's shoes was really the exact opposite of appreciated.

I sighed. "Just open it, will you?"

"You're going to have to take these back to the store," she said, as she removed the lid. "I'd be too embarrassed to be seen with them."

Then she looked down and saw what was inside. Her eyes widened.

"I couldn't get everything," I said quickly. But among other things, I'd found some photographs, a spreadsheet that seemed to be about clothing, some concert stubs, and a tiny scrap of fabric, now stained with soda, that I thought might be her Homecoming Queen sash souvenir. "There might even be more in the bags I managed to grab, but I wasn't sure what was important and—"

She clutched the box to her chest and threw her free arm around my neck. She was crying again, harder than before, and it shook her body.

I found myself pulled down toward her, my nose pressed into the soft skin of her neck. She smelled of flowers and vanilla, a fresh sweet scent that was neither Alona nor Lily, but some combination of the two that resulted in something— and possibly someone—new. I wrapped my arms around as much of her as I could reach. The angle was odd with her lower to the ground than I was.

"Thank you," she said quietly, in a tear-thickened voice.

I touched her shiny brown hair, smoothed it down. It

was not Alona's, not the same at all, but it felt good, right somehow, too. "You're welcome." I hesitated. "I don't know what to call you. I mean, I know who you are, but I can't go around calling you by your real name and—"

She nodded and released me, backing up a step and wiping her face. "I've got them calling me Ally. It sounds close enough to L. E., and apparently Elizabeth is Lily's middle name, so that works out okay. And right now, they're happy enough to call me anything I want." She smiled sadly.

I touched her cheek, my fingers drawn irresistibly to her scar, a symbol of the event that had seemingly kicked all of this into motion, long before we ever knew it was anything more than a single tragic moment in time, unrelated and unconnected to anything before or after it.

She turned away from me slightly, letting her hair slide forward to hide her face. But some impulse led my hand forward to tuck her hair behind her ear again and then to duck in further and press a kiss against her scarred cheek. The skin was slightly raised there but otherwise warm and smooth and tasting of salt from her tears.

Her eyes were wide and brown, but the surprise in them was all Alona. Of course, if she hated imperfections in others, she'd never tolerate them in herself, even a temporary loaner version. "Thank you for saving her," I said. "And for saving you."

She looked away. "I don't know."

"I do," I said firmly. "It's going to be okay."

She looked to me, seeking certainty in my expression, I

think. But then her gaze dropped to my mouth, and in that second, I wanted nothing more than to lean forward and kiss her. But I resisted. It wasn't right. Not yet.

"Ally, honey, are you up? I thought you were resting," Mrs. Turner's voice drifted toward me.

"It's not going to be okay if she catches you down here," she hissed, looking back over her shoulder at the door. "You better go."

"Since when do you care about what a parent thinks?" I asked.

She lifted a shoulder in a shrug. "Since they started caring about me, I guess."

Interesting. One more unexpected change in her. "I'm coming back tomorrow," I warned. "And every day after that, until they let me see you."

She smiled then, a wicked sparkle in her eyes, shades of her former self. "Nice. I like a little desperation in a guy. It builds character."

Good thing. Because I had the feeling by the time this was all over and done with, I'd probably have character— desperation—to spare.

But I wasn't going to worry about that now. I helped her lower the screen and the window, our fingers brushing once more with that same heat as before, and then I left before Mrs. Turner could catch me. I needed to make a good impression tomorrow, the next day, and for however long after that it took to get and keep Alona . . . Ally in my life. It just wasn't the same without her.

❧ ACKNOWLEDGMENTS ❧

Thanks to: my editor, Christian Trimmer, for seeing this book in the chaos that was the previous draft and helping me find it. You are awesome, and I'm so very grateful to be working with you. • Everyone at Hyperion for all the hard work you do. • My agent, Laura Bradford, for always being so calm and confident. • Linnea Sinclair for critiquing this book on a crazy schedule and continually providing much-needed sanity and wisdom. • My first readers—Ed and Debbie Brown, Becky Douthitt, and my fabulous sister, Susan Barnes. • Ryan Turner for helping me figure out Will's college fate. • Age and Dana Tabion for listening, encouraging, and providing the world's best mashed potatoes. • My in-laws, Sue and Dale, for their unwavering support. • My husband, Greg, for loving me even on the days when the writing is not going well and I'm impossible to live with. •

And finally, thank you to everyone who e-mailed, Face-booked (yes, that's a word!), or tweeted to say how much you love Will and Alona. I so appreciate that. You guys rock!